Brander Matthews, Henry Cuyler Bunner

In Partnership

Brander Matthews, Henry Cuyler Bunner

In Partnership

ISBN/EAN: 9783337366148

Printed in Europe, USA, Canada, Australia, Japan

Cover: Foto ©Andreas Hilbeck / pixelio.de

More available books at **www.hansebooks.com**

IN PARTNERSHIP

STUDIES IN STORY-TELLING

By BRANDER MATTHEWS and H. C. BUNNER

NEW YORK

CHARLES SCRIBNER'S SONS

1884

CONTENTS.

                                                    PAGE

THE DOCUMENTS IN THE CASE 3
    By Brander Matthews and H. C. Bunner.

VENETIAN GLASS 48
       By Brander Matthews.

THE RED SILK HANDKERCHIEF 73
       By H. C. Bunner.

THE SEVEN CONVERSATIONS OF DEAR JONES AND
    BABY VAN RENSSELAER 115
       By Brander Matthews and H. C. Bunner.

THE RIVAL GHOSTS 139
       By Brander Matthews.

A LETTER AND A PARAGRAPH 165
       By H. C. Bunner.

PLAYING A PART 179
       By Brander Matthews.

LOVE IN OLD CLOATHES 196
       By H. C. Bunner.

IN PARTNERSHIP.

THE DOCUMENTS IN THE CASE.

BY

BRANDER MATTHEWS AND H. C. BUNNER.

PART FIRST.

Document No. 1.

Paragraph from the "Illustrated London News," published under the head of "Obituary of Eminent Persons," in the issue of January 4th, 1879:

SIR WILLIAM BEAUVOIR, BART.

Sir William Beauvoir, Bart., whose lamented death has just occurred at Brighton, on December 28th, was the head and representative of the junior branch of the very ancient and honourable family of Beauvoir, and was the only son of the late General Sir William Beauvoir, Bart., by his wife Anne, daughter of Colonel Doyle, of Chelsworth Cottage, Suffolk. He was born in 1805, and was educated at Eton and Trinity Hall, Cambridge. He was M. P. for Lancashire from 1837 to 1847, and was appointed a Gentleman of the Privy

3

Chamber in 1843. Sir William married, in 1826, Henrietta Georgiana, fourth daughter of the Right Honourable Adolphus Liddell, Q. C., by whom he had two sons, William Beauvoir and Oliver Liddell Beauvoir. The latter was with his lamented parent when he died. Of the former nothing has been heard for nearly thirty years, about which time he left England suddenly for America. It is supposed that he went to California, shortly after the discovery of gold. Much forgotten gossip will now in all probability be revived, for the will of the lamented baronet has been proved, on the 2d inst., and the personalty sworn under £70,000. The two sons are appointed executors. The estate in Lancashire is left to the elder, and the rest is divided between the brothers. The doubt as to the career of Sir William's eldest son must now of course be cleared up.

This family of Beauvoirs is of Norman descent, and of great antiquity. This is the younger branch, founded in the last century by Sir William Beauvoir, Bart., who was Chief Justice of the Canadas, whence he was granted the punning arms and motto now borne by his descendants — a beaver sable rampant on a field gules; motto, "Damno."

PART SECOND.

Document No. 2.

Promises to pay, put forth by William Beauvoir, junior, at various times in 1848:

I. O. U.

£105. 0. 0.

April 10th, 1848.

William Beauvoir, junr.

Document No. 3.
The same.

I. O. U.

£250. 0. 0.

April 22d, 1848.

William Beauvoir, junr.

Document No. 4.
The same.

I. O. U.

£600. 0. 0.

May 10th, 1848.

William Beauvoir, junr.

Document No. 5.

Extract from the "Sunday Satirist," a journal of high-life, published in London, May 13th, 1848:

Are not our hereditary lawmakers and the members of our old families the guardians of the honour of this realm? One would not think so to see the reckless gait at which some of them go down the road to ruin. The D——e of D——m and the E——l of B——n and L——d Y——g, — are not these pretty guardians of a nation's name? *Quis custodiet?* etc. Guardians, forsooth, *parce qu'ils se sont donnés la peine de naître!* Some of the gentry make the running as well as their betters. Young W——m B——r, son of old Sir W——m B——r, late M. P. for L——e, is a truly model young man. He comes of a good old county family — his mother was a daughter of the Right Honourable A——s L——l, and he himself is old enough to know better. But we hear of his escapades night after night, and day after day. He bets all day and he plays all night, and poor tired nature has to make the best of it. And his poor worn purse gets the worst of it. He has duns by the score. His I. O. U.'s are held by every Jew in the city. He is not content with a little gentlemanlike game of whist or *écarté*, but he must needs revive for his special use and behoof the dangerous and well-nigh forgotten *pharaoh*. As luck would have it, he had lost as much at this game of brute chance as ever he would at any game of skill. His judgment of horseflesh is no better than his luck at cards. He came a cropper over the "Two Thousand

Guineas." The victory of the favourite cost him to the tune of over six thousand pounds. We learn that he hopes to recoup himself on the Derby, by backing Shylock for nearly nine thousand pounds; one bet was twelve hundred guineas.

And this is the sort of man who may be chosen at any time by force of family interest to make laws for the toiling millions of Great Britain!

Document No. 6.

Extract from "Bell's Life" of May 19th, 1848:

THE DERBY DAY.

WEDNESDAY. — This day, like its predecessor, opened with a cloudless sky, and the throng which crowded the avenues leading to the grand scene of attraction was, as we have elsewhere remarked, incalculable.

. . . .

THE DERBY.

The Derby Stakes of 50 sovs. each, h. ft. for three-year-olds; colts, 8 st. 7 lb., fillies, 8 st. 2 lb.; the second to receive 100 sovs., and the winner to pay 100 sovs. towards police, etc.; mile and a half on the new Derby course; 215 subs.

Lord Clifden's b. c. *Surplice*, by Touchstone . . .	1
Mr. Bowe's b. c. *Springy Jack*, by Hetman . . .	2
Mr. B. Green's br. c. *Shylock*, by Simoon	3
Mr. Payne's b. c. *Glendower*, by Slane	0
Mr. J. P. Day's b. c. *Nil Desperandum*, by Venison .	0

. . . .

Document No. 7.

Paragraph of Shipping Intelligence from the " Liverpool Courier" of June 21st, 1848:

The bark *Euterpe*, Captain Riding, belonging to the Transatlantic Clipper Line of Messrs. Judkins & Cooke, left the Mersey yesterday afternoon, bound for New York. She took out the usual complement of steerage passengers. The first officer's cabin is occupied by Professor Titus Peebles, M. R. C. S., M. R. G. S., lately instructor in metallurgy at the University of Edinburgh, and Mr. William Beauvoir. Professor Peebles, we are informed, has an important scientific mission in the States, and will not return for six months.

Document No. 8.

Paragraph from the " N. Y. Herald" of September 9th, 1848.

While we well know that the record of vice and dissipation can never be pleasing to the refined tastes of the cultivated denizens of the only morally pure metropolis on the face of the earth, yet it may be of interest to those who enjoy the fascinating study of human folly and frailty to "point a moral or adorn a tale" from the events transpiring in our very midst. Such as these will view with alarm the sad example afforded the youth of our city by the dissolute career of a young lump of aristocratic affectation and patrician profligacy, recently arrived in this city. This young *gentleman's* (save the mark!) name is Lord

William F. Beauvoir, the latest scion of a venerable and wealthy English family. We print the full name of this beautiful exemplar of "haughty Albion," although he first appeared among our citizens under the alias of Beaver, by which name he is now generally known, although recorded on the books of the Astor House by the name which our enterprise first gives to the public. Lord Beauvoir's career since his arrival here has been one of unexampled extravagance and mad immorality. His days and nights have been passed in the gilded palaces of the fickle goddess, Fortune, in Thomas Street and College Place, where he has squandered fabulous sums, by some stated to amount to over £78,000 sterling. It is satisfactory to know that retribution has at last overtaken him. His enormous income has been exhausted to the ultimate farthing, and at latest accounts he had quit the city, leaving behind him, it is shrewdly suspected, a large hotel bill, though no such admission can be extorted from his last landlord, who is evidently a sycophantic adulator of British "aristocracy."

𝔇ocument 𝔑o. 9.

Certificate of deposit, vulgarly known as a pawn-ticket, issued by one Simpson to William Beauvoir, December 2d, 1848.

John Simpson,
>> **Loan Office,**
>>> **36 Bowery,**
>>>> **New York.**

Dec. 2d, 1848.

	Dolls.	Cts.
One Gold Hunting-case Watch and Chain,	*150*	*00*
William Beauvoir.		

Not accountable in case of fire, damage, moth, robbery, breakage, &c.
25% per ann.   Good for 1 year only.

𝔇ocument 𝔑o. 10.

Letter from the late John Phœnix, found among the posthumous papers of the late John P. Squibob, and promptly published in the " San Diego Herald."

OFF THE COAST OF FLORIDA, Jan. 3, 1849.

MY DEAR SQUIB : — I imagine your pathetic inquiry as to my whereabouts — pathetic, not to say hypo-thetic — for I am now where I cannot hear the dulcet strains of your voice. I am on board ship. I am half seas over. I am bound for California by way of the Isthmus. I am going for the gold, my boy, the gold. In the mean time I am lying around loose on the deck of this magnificent vessel, the *Mercy G. Tarbox,* of

Nantucket, bred by *Noah's Ark* out of *Pilot-boat*, dam by *Mudscow* out of *Raging Canawl*. The *Mercy G. Turbox* is one of the best boats of Nantucket, and Captain Clearstarch is one of the best captains all along shore — although, friend Squibob, I feel sure that you are about to observe that a captain with a name like that would give anyone the blues. But don't do it, Squib! Spare me this once.

But as a matter of fact this ultramarine joke of yours is about cast. It was blue on the *Mercy G.* — mighty blue, too. And it needed the inspiring hope of the gold I was soon to pick up in nuggets to stiffen my backbone to a respectable degree of rigidity. I was about ready to wilt. But I discovered two Englishmen on board, and now I get along all right. We have formed a little temperance society — just we three, you know — to see if we cannot, by a course of sampling and severe study, discover which of the captain's liquors is most dangerous, so that we can take the pledge not to touch it. One of them is a chemist or a metallurgist, or something scientific. The other is a gentleman.

The chemist or metallurgist or something scientific is Professor Titus Peebles, who is going out to prospect for gold. He feels sure that his professional training will give him the inside track in the gulches and gold mines. He is a smart chap. He invented the celebrated "William Riley Baking Powder" — bound to rise up every time.

And here I must tell you a little circumstance. As I was coming down to the dock in New York, to go

aboard the *Mercy G.*, a small boy was walloping a boy
still smaller; so I made peace, and walloped them both.
And then they both began heaving rocks at me —
one of which I caught dexterously in the dexter hand.
Yesterday, as I was pacing the deck with the professor,
I put my hand in my pocket and found this stone. So
I asked the professor what it was.

He looked at it and said it was gneiss.

"Is it?" said I. "Well, if a small but energetic
youth had taken you on the back of the head with it,
you would not think it so nice!"

And then, O Squib, he set out to explain that he
meant "gneiss," not "nice!" The ignorance of these
English about a joke is really wonderful. It is easy
to see that they have never been brought up on them.
But perhaps there was some excuse for the professor
that day, for he was the president *pro tem.* of our pro-
jected temperance society, and as such he had been
making a quantitative and qualitative analysis of another
kind of quartz.

So much for the chemist or metallurgist or something
scientific. The gentleman and I get on better. His
name is Beaver, which he persists in spelling Beauvoir.
Ridiculous, is n't it? How easy it is to see that the
English have never had the advantage of a good
common-school education — so few of them can spell.
Here's a man don't know how to spell his own name.
And this shows how the race over there on the little
island is degenerating. It was not so in other days.
Shakspere, for instance, not only knew how to spell
his own name, but — and this is another proof of his

superiority to his contemporaries — he could spell it in half a dozen different ways.

This Beaver is a clever fellow, and we get on first rate together. He is going to California for gold — like the rest of us. But I think he has had his share — and spent it. At any rate he has not much now. I have been teaching him poker, and I am afraid he won't have any soon. I have an idea he has been going pretty fast — and mostly down hill. But he has his good points. He is a gentleman all through, as you can see. Yes, friend Squibob, even you could see right through him. We are all going to California together, and I wonder which one of the three will turn up trumps first — Beaver, or the chemist, metallurgist or something scientific, or

Yours respectfully, JOHN PHŒNIX.

P. S. — You think this a stupid letter, perhaps, and not interesting. Just reflect on my surroundings. Besides, the interest will accumulate a good while before you get the missive. And I don't know how you ever are to get it, for there is no post-office near here, and on the Isthmus the mails are as uncertain as the females are everywhere. (I am informed that there is no postage on old jokes — so I let that stand.) J. P.

Document No. 11.

Extract from the "Bone Gulch Palladium," June 3d, 1850:

Our readers may remember hovv frequeñtly vve have declared our firm belief iñ the future uñexampled

prosperity of Boñe Gulch.   VVe savv it iñ the immediate future the metropolis of the Pacific Slope, as it was
iñtended by nature to be.   VVe poiñted out repeatedly
that a time vvould come vvheñ Boñe Gulch would be
an emporium of the arts añd scieñces añd of the best
society, eveñ more thañ it is novv.   VVe foresavv the
time vvheñ the best meñ from the old cities of the
East vvould come flockiñg to us, passiñg vvith coñ-
tempt the puñy settlemeñt of Deadhorse.   But eveñ
vve did not so sooñ see that members of the aristocracy of the effete moñarchies of despotic Europe vvould
ackñovvledge the uñdeniable advañtages of Boñe
Gulch, añd come here to stay permañently añd forever.   VVithiñ the past vveek vve have received here
Hoñ. VVilliam Beaver, oñe of the first men of Great
Britain añd Irelañd, a statesmañ, añ orator, a soldier,
añd añ exteñsive traveller.   He has come to Boñe
Gulch as the best spot oñ the face of the everlasting
uñiverse.   It is ñeedless to say that our promiñeñt
citizeñs have received him with great cordiality.   Boñe
Gulch is not like Deadhorse.   VVe kñovv a geñtlemañ
vvheñ vve see oñe.

Hoñ. Mr. Beaver is oñe of ñature's ñoblemeñ; he is
also related to the Royal Family of Englañd.   He is a
secoñd cousiñ of the Queeñ, and boards at the Tovver
of Loñdoñ vvith her vvheñ at home.   VVe are iñ-
formed that he has frequently takeñ the Priñce of
VVales out for a ride iñ his baby-vvagoñ.

VVe take great pleasure iñ coñgratulating Boñe
Gulch oñ its latest acquisitioñ.   Añd we knovv Hoñ.
Mr. Beaver is sure to get along all right here uñder

the best climate iñ the vvorld añd vvith the ñoblest men the sun ever shoñe oñ.

Document No. 12.

Extract from the Dead Horse "Gazette and Courier of Civilization" of August 26th, 1850:

BONEGULCH'S BRITISHER.

Bonegulch sits in sackcloth and ashes and cools her mammoth cheek in the breezes of Colorado canyon. The self-styled Emporium of the West has lost her British darling, Beaver Bill, the big swell who was first cousin to the Marquis of Buckingham and own grandmother to the Emperor of China, the man with the biled shirt and low-necked shoes. This curled darling of the Bonegulch aristocrat-worshippers passed through Deadhorse yesterday, clean bust. Those who remember how the four-fingered editor of the Bonegulch "Palladium" pricked up his ears and lifted up his falsetto crow when this lovely specimen of the British snob first honored him by striking him for a $ will appreciate the point of the joke.

It is said that the "Palladium" is going to come out, when it makes its next semi-occasional appearance, in full mourning, with turned rules. For this festive occasion we offer Brother B. the use of our late retired Spanish font, which we have discarded for the new and elegant dress in which we appear to-day, and to which we have elsewhere called the attention of our readers. It will be a change for the "Palladium's" eleven unhappy readers, who are getting very tired of the old

type cast for the Concha Mission in 1811, which tries
to make up for its lack of w's by a plentiful superfluity
of greaser u's.   How are you, Brother Biles?

"We don't know a gent when we see him."   Oh
no (?)!

Document No. 13.

*Paragraph from "Police Court Notes," in the New
Centreville [late Dead Horse] Evening Gazette,"
January 2d, 1858:*

HYMENEAL HIGH JINKS.

William Beaver, better known ten years ago as
"Beaver Bill," is now a quiet and prosperous agricul-
turalist in the Steal Valley.   He was, however, a
pioneer in the 1849 movement, and a vivid memory of
this fact at times moves him to quit his bucolic labors
and come in town for a real old-fashioned tare.   He
arrived in New Centreville during Christmas week;
and got married suddenly, but not unexpectedly, yesterday morning.   His friends took it upon themselves
to celebrate the joyful occasion, rare in the experience
of at least one of the parties, by getting very high on
Irish Ike's whiskey and serenading the newly-married
couple with fish-horns, horse-fiddles, and other impro-
vised musical instruments.   Six of the participators in
this epithalamial serenade, namely, José Tanco, Hiram
Scuttles, John P. Jones, Hermann Bumgardner, Jean
Durant ("Frenchy"), and Bernard McGinnis ("Big
Barney"), were taken in tow by the police force, assisted
by citizens, and locked up over night, to cool their generous enthusiasm in the gloomy dungeons of Justice

Skinner's calaboose. This morning all were discharged with a reprimand, except Big Barney and José Tanco, who, being still drunk, were allotted ten days in default of $10. The bridal pair left this noon for the bridegroom's ranch.

𝔇ocument 𝔑o. 14.

Extract from "The New York Herald" for June 23d, 1861:

THE RED SKINS.

———

A BORDER WAR AT LAST!

———

INDIAN INSURRECTION.

———

RED DEVILS RISING!

———

WOMEN AND CHILDREN SEEKING SAFETY IN THE LARGER TOWNS.

———

HORRIBLE HOLOCAUSTS ANTICIPATED.

———

BURYING THE HATCHET — IN THE WHITE MAN'S HEAD.

———

[SPECIAL DESPATCH TO THE NEW YORK HERALD.]

CHICAGO, June 22, 1861.

Great uneasiness exists all along the Indian frontier. Nearly all the regular troops have been withdrawn from the West for service in the South. With the return of the warm weather it seems certain that the red skins will take advantage of the opportunity thus offered, and inaugurate a bitter and vindictive fight against the whites. Rumors come from the agencies that the

Indians are leaving in numbers. A feverish excitement among them has been easily to be detected. Their ponies are now in good condition, and forage can soon be had in abundance on the prairie, if it is not already. Everything points toward a sudden and startling outbreak of hostilities.

[SPECIAL DESPATCH TO THE NEW YORK HERALD.]

ST. PAUL, June 22, 1861.

The Sioux near here are all in a ferment. Experienced Indian fighters say the signs of a speedy going on the war-path are not to be mistaken. No one can tell how soon the whole frontier may be in a bloody blaze. The women and children are rapidly coming in from all exposed settlements. Nothing overt as yet has transpired, but that the Indians will collide very soon with the settlers is certain. All the troops have been withdrawn. In our defenceless state there is no knowing how many lives may be lost before the regiments of volunteers now organizing can take the field.

LATER.

THE WAR BEGUN.

FIRST BLOOD FOR THE INDIANS.

THE SCALPING KNIFE AND THE TOMAHAWK AT WORK AGAIN.

[SPECIAL DESPATCH TO THE NEW YORK HERALD.]

BLACK WING AGENCY, June 22, 1861.

The Indians made a sudden and unexpected attack on the town of Coyote Hill, forty miles from here, last night, and did much damage before the surprised settlers rallied and drove them off. The red skins met with heavy losses. Among the whites killed are a man named William Beaver, sometimes called Beaver Bill, and his wife. Their child, a beautiful little girl of two, was carried off by the red rascals. A party has been made up to pursue them. Owing to their taking their wounded with them, the trail is very distinct.

Document No. 15.

Letter from Mrs. Edgar Saville, in San Francisco, to Mr. Edgar Saville, in Chicago.

CAL. JARDINE'S

MONSTER VARIETY AND DRAMATIC COMBINATION.

ON THE ROAD.

G. W. K. McCULLUM, *Treasurer.*	*No dates filled except with first-class houses.*
HI. SAMUELS, *Stage Manager.*	
JNO. SHANKS, *Advance.*	*Hall owners will please consider silence a polite negative.*

SAN FRANCISCO, January 29, 1863.

MY DEAR OLD MAN! — Here we are in our second week at Frisco and you will be glad to know playing to steadily increasing biz, having signed for two weeks more, certain. I didn't like to mention it when I wrote you last, but things were very queer after we left Denver, and "Treasury" was a mockery till we got to Bluefoot Springs, which is a mining town, where we showed in the hotel dining-room. Then there was a

strike just before the curtain went up. The house was
mostly miners in red shirts and very exacting. The
sinews were forthcoming very quick my dear, and after
that the ghost walked quite regular. So now everything is bright, and you won't have to worry if Chicago
does n't do the right thing by you.

I don't find this engagement half as disagreeable as
I expected. Of course it ain't so very nice travelling
in a combination with variety talent but they keep to
themselves and we regular professionals make a *happy
family* that Barnum would not be ashamed of and
quite separate and comfortable. We don't associate
with any of them only with The Unique Mulligans
wife, because he beats her. So when he is on a regular
she sleeps with me.

And talking of liquor dear old man, if you knew
how glad and proud I was to see you writing so
straight and steady and beautiful in your three last
letters. O, I'm sure my darling if the boys thought of
the little wife out on the road they would n't plague
you so with the Enemy. Tell Harry Atkinson this
from me, he has a good kind heart but he is the worst
of your friends. Every night when I am dressing I
think of you at Chicago, and pray you may never
again go on the way you did that terrible night at
Rochester. Tell me dear, did you look handsome in
Horatio? You ought to have had Laertes instead of
that duffing Merivale.

And now I have the queerest thing to tell you.
Jardine is going in for Indians and has secured six
very ugly ones. I mean real Indians, not professional.

They are hostile Comanshies or something who have just laid down their arms. They had an insurrection in the first year of the War, when the troops went East, and they killed all the settlers and ranches and destroyed the canyons somewhere out in Nevada, and when they were brought here they had a wee little kid with them only four or five years old, but *so sweet.* They stole her and killed her parents and brought her up for their own in the cunningest little moccasins. She could not speak a word of English except her own name which is Nina. She has blue eyes and all her second teeth. The ladies here made a great fuss about her and sent her flowers and worsted afgans, but they did not do anything else for her and left her to us.

O dear old man you must let me have her! You never refused me a thing yet and she is so like our Avonia Marie that my heart almost breaks when she puts her arms around my neck — *she calls me mamma already.* I want to have her with us when we get the little farm — and it must be near, that little farm of ours — we have waited for it so long — and something tells me my own old faker will make his hit soon and be great. You can't tell how I have loved it and hoped for it and how real every foot of that farm is to me. And though I can never see my own darling's face among the roses it will make me so happy to see this poor dead mother's pet get red and rosy in the country air. And till the farm comes we shall always have enough for her, without your ever having to black up again as you did for me the winter I was sick my own poor boy!

Write me yes — you will be glad when you see her. And now love and regards to Mrs. Barry and all friends. Tell the Worst of Managers that he knows where to find his leading juvenile for next season. Think how funny it would be for us to play together next year — we have n't done it since '57 — the third year we were married. That was my first season higher than walking — and now I'm quite an old woman — most thirty dear!

Write me soon a letter like that last one — and send a kiss to Nina — *our Nina.*

Your own girl,

MARY.

P. S.   He has not worried me since.

Nina drew this herself she says it is a horse so that you can get here soon.

PART THIRD.

Document No. 16.

Letter from Messrs. Throstlethwaite, Throstlethwaite, and Dick, Solicitors, Lincoln's Inn, London, England, to Messrs. Hitchcock and Van Rensselaer, Attorneys and Counsellors at Law, 76 Broadway, New York, U. S. A.

January 8, 1879.

Messrs. HITCHCOCK & VAN RENSSELAER:

GENTLEMEN: On the death of our late client, Sir William Beauvoir, Bart., and after the reading of the deceased gentleman's will, drawn up nearly forty years ago by our Mr. Dick, we were requested by Oliver Beauvoir, Esq., the second son of the late Sir William, to assist him in discovering and communicating with his elder brother, the present Sir William Beauvoir, of whose domicile we have little or no information.

After a consultation between Mr. Oliver Beauvoir and our Mr. Dick, it was seen that the sole knowledge in our possession amounted substantially to this: Thirty years ago the elder son of the late baronet, after indulging in dissipation in every possible form, much to the sorrow of his respected parent, who frequently expressed as much to our Mr. Dick, disappeared, leaving behind him bills and debts of all descriptions, which we, under instructions from Sir William, examined, audited, and paid. Sir William Beauvoir would allow no search to be made for his erring son and would listen to no mention of his name. Current gossip declared that he had gone to New York, where he probably arrived about midsummer, 1848. Mr. Oliver Beauvoir thinks that he crossed to the States in company with a distinguished scientific gentleman, Professor Titus Peebles. Within a year after his departure news came that he had gone to California with Professor Peebles; this was about the time gold was discovered in the States. That the present Sir William Beauvoir did about this time actually arrive on the Pacific Coast in company with the distinguished scientific man above mentioned, we have every reason to believe : we have even direct evidence on the subject. A former junior clerk, who had left us at about the same period as the disappearance of the elder son of our late client, accosted our Mr. Dick when the latter was in Paris last summer, and informed him (our Mr. Dick) that he (the former junior clerk) was now a resident of Nevada and a member of Congress for that county, and in the course of conversation he mentioned that he had seen Professor Peebles and the son of our late client in San Francisco, nearly thirty years ago. Other information we have none. It ought not to be difficult to discover Professor Peebles, whose scientific attainments have doubtless ere this been duly recognized by the U. S. government. As our late client leaves the valuable family estate in Lancashire to his elder son and divides the remainder equally between his two sons, you will readily see why we invoke your assistance in discovering the present domicile of the late baronet's elder son, or, in default thereof, in placing in our hand such proof of his death as may be necessary to establish that lamentable fact in our probate court.

We have the honour to remain, as ever, your most humble and obedient servants,

THROSTLETHWAITE, THROSTLETHWAITE, & DICK.

P. S. — Our late client's grandson, Mr. William Beauvoir, the only child of Oliver Beauvoir, Esq., is now in the States, in Chicago or Nebraska or somewhere in the West. We shall be pleased if you can keep him informed as to the progress of your investigations. Our Mr. Dick has requested Mr. Oliver Beauvoir to give his son your address, and to suggest his calling on you as he passes through New York on his way home. T. T. & D.

Document No. 17.

Letter from Messrs. Hitchcock and Van Rensselaer, New York, to Messrs. Pixley and Sutton, Attorneys and Counsellors at Law, 98 California Street, San Francisco, California.

Law Offices of Hitchcock & Van Rensselaer,
76 Broadway, New York.
P. O. Box 4076.

Jan. 22, 1879.

Messrs. PIXLEY AND SUTTON:

GENTLEMEN: We have just received from our London correspondents, Messrs. Throstlethwaite, Throstlethwaite, and Dick, of Lincoln's Inn, London, the letter, a copy of which is herewith enclosed, to which we invite your attention. We request that you will do

all in your power to aid us in the search for the miss-
ing Englishman. From the letter of Messrs. Throstlethwaite, Throstlethwaite, and Dick, it seems extremely
probable, not to say certain, that Mr. Beauvoir arrived
in your city about 1849, in company with a distinguished English scientist, Professor Titus Peebles,
whose professional attainments were such that he is
probably well known, if not in California, at least in
some other of the mining States. The first thing to
be done, therefore, it seems to us, is to ascertain the
whereabouts of the professor, and to interview him at
once. It may be that he has no knowledge of the
present domicile of Mr. William Beauvoir, in which
case we shall rely on you to take such steps as, in your
judgment, will best conduce to a satisfactory solution
of the mystery. In any event, please look up Professor Peebles, and interview him at once.

Pray keep us fully informed by telegraph of your
movements.   Yr obt serv'ts,
             HITCHCOCK & VAN RENSSELAER.

Document No. 18.

*Telegram from Messrs. Pixley and Sutton, Attorneys
and Counsellors at Law, 98 California Street, San
Francisco, California, to Messrs. Hitchcock and
Van Rensselaer, Attorneys and Counsellors at Law,
76 Broadway, New York.*

SAN FRANCISCO, CAL., Jan. 30.

Tite Peebles well known frisco not professor keeps
faro bank.   PIXLEY & SUTTON.   (D. H. 919.)

Document No. 19.

Telegram from Messrs. Hitchcock and Van Rensselaer to Messrs. Pixley and Sutton, in answer to the preceding.

NEW YORK, Jan. 30.

Must be mistake Titus Peebles distinguished scientist.

HITCHCOCK & VAN RENSSELAER.

(Free.   Answer to D. H.)

Document No. 20.

Telegram from Messrs. Pixley and Sutton to Messrs. Hitchcock and Van Rensselaer, in reply to the preceding.

SAN FRANCISCO, CAL., Jan. 30.

No mistake distinguished faro banker suspected skin game shall we interview.

PIXLEY & SUTTON.   (D. H. 919.)

Document No. 21.

Telegram from Messrs. Hitchcock and Van Rensselaer to Messrs. Pixley and Sutton, in reply to the preceding.

NEW YORK, Jan. 30.

Must be mistake interview anyway.

HITCHCOCK & VAN RENSSELAER.

(Free.   Answer to D. H.)

Document No. 22.

Telegram from Messrs. Pixley & Sutton to Messrs. Hitchcock and Van Rensselaer, in reply to the preceding.

SAN FRANCISCO, CAL., Jan. 30.

Peebles out of town have written him.

PIXLEY & SUTTON.   (D. II. 919.)

Document No. 23.

Letter from Tite W. Peebles, delegate to the California Constitutional Convention, Sacramento, to Messrs. Pixley and Sutton, 98 California Street, San Francisco, California.

SACRAMENTO, Feb. 2, '79.

Messrs. PIXLEY & SUTTON:

San Francisco.

GENTLEMEN: Your favor of the 31st ult., forwarded me from San Francisco, has been duly rec'd, and contents thereof noted.

My time is at present so fully occupied by my duties as a delegate to the Constitutional Convention that I can only jot down a brief report of my recollections on this head. When I return to S. F., I shall be happy to give you any further information that may be in my possession.

The person concerning whom you inquire was my fellow passenger on my first voyage to this State on board the *Mercy G. Tarbox*, in the latter part of the year. He was then known as Mr. William Beauvoir. I was acquainted with his history, of which the details escape me at this writing. He was a countryman of mine; a member of an important county family — Devonian, I believe — and had left England on account of large gambling debts, of which he confided to me the exact figure. I believe they totted up something like £14,500.

I had at no time a very intimate acquaintance with Mr. Beauvoir; during our sojourn on the *Tarbox* he was the chosen associate of a depraved and vicious character named Phœnix. I am not averse from saying that I was then a member of a profession rather different to my present one, being, in fact, professor of metallurgy, and I saw much less, at that period, of Mr. B. than I probably should now.

Directly we landed at S. F., the object of your inquiries set out for the gold region, without adequate preparation, like so many others did at that time, and, I heard, fared very ill.

I encountered him some six months later; I have forgotten precisely in what locality, though I have a faint impression that his then habitat was some cañon or ravine deriving its name from certain osseous deposits. Here he had engaged in the business of gold-mining, without, perhaps, sufficient grounds for any confident hope of ultimate success. I have his I. O. U. for the amount of my fee for assaying several specimens from his claim, said specimens being all iron pyrites.

This is all I am able to call to mind at present in the matter of Mr. Beauvoir. I trust his subsequent career was of a nature better calculated to be satisfactory to himself; but his mineralogical knowledge was but superficial; and his character was sadly deformed by a fatal taste for low associates.

I remain, gentlemen, your very humble and obd't servant, Titus W. Peebles.

P. S. — Private.

My dear Pix: If you don't feel inclined to pony up that little sum you are out on the bay gelding, drop down to my place when I get back and I'll give you another chance for your life at the pasteboards. Constitution going through.

Yours,   TITE.

PART FOURTH.

Document No. 24.

Extract from the New Centreville [late Dead Horse] "Gazette and Courier of Civilization," December 20th, 1878:

"Miss Nina Saville appeared last night at the Mendocino Grand Opera House, in her unrivalled specialty of *Winona, the Child of the Prairies;* supported by Tompkins and Frobisher's Grand Stellar Constellation. Although Miss Saville has long been known as one of the most promising of California's younger tragediennes, we feel safe in saying that the impression she produced upon the large and cultured audience gathered to greet her last night stamped her as one of the greatest and most phenomenal geniuses of our own or other times. Her marvellous beauty of form and feature, added to her wonderful artistic power, and her perfect mastery of the difficult science of clog-dancing, won her an immediate place in the hearts of our citizens, and confirmed the belief that California need no longer look to Europe or Chicago for dramatic talent of the highest order. The sylph-like beauty, the harmonious and ever-varying grace, the vivacity and the power of the young artist who made her maiden effort among us last night, prove conclusively that the virgin soil of California teems with yet undiscovered fires of genius. The drama of *Winona, the Child of the Prairies*, is a pure, refined, and thoroughly absorbing entertainment, and has been pronounced by the entire press of the country equal to if not superior to the fascinating *Lady of Lyons*. It introduces all the favorites of the company in new and original characters, and with its original music, which is a prominent feature, has already received over 200 representations in the principal cities in the country. It abounds in effective situations, striking tableaux, and a most quaint and original concert entitled 'The Mule Fling,' which alone is worth the price of admission. As this is the first presentation in this city, the theatre will no doubt be crowded, and seats should be secured early in the day. The drama will be preceded by that prince of humorists, Mr. Billy Barker, in his humorous sketches and pictures from life.''

We quote the above from our esteemed contemporary, the Mendocino *Gazette*, at the request of Mr. Zeke Kilburn, Miss Saville's advance agent, who has still further appealed to us, not only on the ground of our common humanity, but as the only appreciative and thoroughly informed critics on the Pacific Slope to "endorse" this rather vivid expression of opinion. Nothing will give us greater pleasure. Allowing for the habitual enthusiasm of our northern neighbor, and for the well-known chaste aridity of Mendocino in respect of female beauty, we have no doubt that Miss Nina Saville is all that the fancy, peculiarly opulent and active even for an advance agent, of Mr. Kilburn has painted her, and is quite such a vision of youth, beauty, and artistic phenomenality as will make the stars of Paris and Illinois pale their ineffectual fires. Miss Saville will appear in her "unrivalled specialty" at Hank's New Centreville Opera House, to-morrow night, as may be gathered, in a general way, from an advertisement in another column.

We should not omit to mention that Mr. Zeke Kilburn, Miss Saville's advance agent, is a gentleman of imposing presence, elegant manners, and complete knowledge of his business. This information may be relied upon as at least authentic, having been derived from Mr. Kilburn himself, to which we can add, as our own contribution, the statement that Mr. Kilburn is a gentleman of marked liberality in his ideas of spirituous refreshments, and of equal originality in his conception of the uses, objects and personal susceptibilities of the journalistic profession.

Document No. 25.

Local item from the " New Centreville Standard," December 20th, 1878 :

Hon. William Beauvoir has registered at the United States Hotel. Mr. Beauvoir is a young English gentleman of great wealth, now engaged in investigating the gigantic resources of this great country. We welcome him to New Centreville.

Document No. 26.

Programme of the performance given in the Centreville Theatre, Dec. 21st, 1878 :

HANKS' NEW CENTREVILLE OPERA HOUSE.

A. JACKSON HANKS..........Sole Proprietor and Manager.

FIRST APPEARANCE IN THIS CITY OF

TOMPKINS & FROBISHER'S

GRAND STELLAR CONSTELLATION,

Supporting California's favorite daughter, the young American
Tragedienne,

MISS NINA SAVILLE,

Who will appear in Her Unrivalled Specialty,

"WINONA, THE CHILD OF THE PRAIRIE."

THIS EVENING, DECEMBER 21st, 1878,

Will be presented, with the following phenomenal cast, the accepted
American Drama.

WINONA, THE CHILD OF THE PRAIRIE.

WINONA .... ⎫
MISS FLORA MacMADISON... ⎟
BIDDY FLAHERTY .... ⎟ **Miss NINA**
OLD AUNT DINAH (with Song, "Don't Get Weary")............... ⎟ **SAVILLE.**
SALLY HOSKINS (with the old-time melody, "Bobbin' Around")........ ⎟
POOR JOE (with Song) .... ⎟
FRAULINE LINA BOOBENSTEIN (with stammering Song, "I yoost landet") ⎭
SIR EDMOND BENNETT (specially engaged) ....E. C. GRAINGER
WALTON TRAVERS .... G. W. PARSONS
GIPSY JOE .... M. ISAACS
'ANNADLE 'ORACE 'IGGINS.................................BILLY BARKER
TOMMY TIPPER...MISS MAMIE SMITH
PETE, the Man on the Dock...................................SI HANCOCK
MRS. MALONE, the Old Woman in the Little House...............MRS. K. Y. BOOTH
ROBERT BENNETT (aged 5)........................... LITTLE ANNIE WATSON

Act I.— The Old Home.   Act II.— Alone in the World.

Act III.— The Frozen Gulf:

THE GREAT ICEBERG SENSATION.

Act IV.— Wedding Bells.

"WINONA, THE CHILD OF THE PRAIRIE," WILL BE PRECEDED BY

A FAVORITE FARCE,

In which the great BILLY BARKER will appear in one of his most out-
rageously funny bits.

NEW SCENERY....................by...................... Q. Z. SLOCUM

Music by Professor Kiddoo's Silver Bugle Brass Band and
Philharmonic Orchestra.

Chickway's Grand Piano, lent by Schmidt, 2 Opera House Block.

AFTER THE SHOW   GO TO HANKS'   AND SEE A MAN!

Pop Williams, the only legitimate Bill-Poster in New Centreville.

(New Centreville Standard Print.)

Extract from the New Centreville [late Dead Horse]
"Gazette and Courier of Civilization," Dec. 24th,
1878.

A little while ago, in noting the arrival of Miss Nina
Saville of the New Centreville Opera House, we quoted
rather extensively from our esteemed contemporary,
the Mendocino *Times,* and commented upon the quotation. Shortly afterwards, it may also be remembered, we made a very direct and decided apology for
the sceptical levity which inspired those remarks, and
expressed our hearty sympathy with the honest, if
somewhat effusive, enthusiasm with which the dramatic
critic of Mendocino greeted the sweet and dainty little
girl who threw over the dull, weary old business of the
stage "sensation" the charm of a fresh and childlike
beauty and originality, as rare and delicate as those
strange, unreasonable little glimmers of spring sunsets
that now and then light up for a brief moment the
dull skies of winter evenings, and seem to have
strayed into ungrateful January out of sheer pity for
the sad earth.

Mendocino noticed the facts that form the basis of
the above meteorological simile, and we believe we
gave Mendocino full credit for it at the time. We
refer to the matter at this date only because in ou.
remarks of a few days ago we had occasion to mention
the fact of the existence of Mr. Zeke Kilburn, an advance agent, who called upon us at the time, to endeavor
to induce us, by means apparently calculated more

closely for the latitude of Mendocino, to extend to Miss Saville, before her appearance, the critical approbation which we gladly extended after. This little item of interest we alluded to at the time, and furthermore intimated, with some vagueness, that there existed in Mr. Kilburn's character a certain misdirected zeal which, combined with a too keen artistic appreciation, are apt to be rather dangerous stock-in-trade for an advance agent.

It was twenty-seven minutes past two o'clock yesterday afternoon. The chaste white mystery of Shigo Mountain was already taking on a faint, almost imperceptible hint of pink, like the warm cheek of a girl who hears a voice and anticipates a blush. Yet the rays of the afternoon sun rested with undiminished radiance on the empty pork-barrel in front of McMullin's shebang. A small and vagrant infant, whose associations with empty barrels were doubtless hitherto connected solely with dreams of saccharine dissipation, approached the bunghole with precocious caution, and retired with celerity and a certain acquisition of experience. An unattached goat, a martyr to the radical theory of personal investigation, followed in the footsteps of infantile humanity, retired with even greater promptitude, and was fain to stay its stomach on a presumably empty rend-rock can, afterward going into seclusion behind McMullin's horse-shed, before the diuretic effect of tin flavored with blasting-powder could be observed by the attentive eye of science.

Mr. Kilburn emerged from the hostelry of McMullin. Mr. Kilburn, as we have before stated at his own request, is a gentleman of imposing presence. It is well that we made this statement when we did, for it is hard to judge of the imposing quality in a gentleman's presence when that gentleman is suspended from the arm of another gentleman by the collar of the first gentleman's coat. The gentleman in the rear of Mr. Kilburn was Mr. William Beauvoir, a young Englishman in a check suit. Mr. Beauvoir is not avowedly a man of imposing presence; he wears a seal ring, and he is generally a scion of an effete oligarchy, but he has, since his introduction into this community, behaved himself, to use the adjectivial adverb of Mr. McMullin, *white*, and he has a very remarkable biceps. These qualities may hereafter enhance his popularity in New Centreville.

Mr. Beauvoir's movements, at twenty-seven minutes past two yesterday afternoon, were few and simple. He doubled Mr. Kilburn up, after the fashion of an ordinary jack-knife, and placed him in the barrel, wedge-extremity first, remarking, as he did so, "She is, is she?" He then rammed Mr. Kilburn carefully home, and put the cover on.

We learn to-day that Mr. Kilburn has resumed his professional duties on the road.

Document No. 28.

Account of the same event from the New Centreville "Standard," December 24th, 1878.

It seems strange that even the holy influences which radiate from this joyous season cannot keep some men from getting into unseemly wrangles. It was only yesterday that our local saw a street row here in the quiet avenues of our peaceful city — a street row recalling the riotous scenes which took place here before Dead Horse experienced a change of heart and became New Centreville. Our local succeeded in gathering all the particulars of the affray, and the following statement is reliable. It seems that Mr. Kilburn, the gentlemanly and affable advance agent of the Nina Saville Dramatic Company, now performing at Andy Hanks' Opera House to big houses, was brutally assaulted by a ruffianly young Englishman, named Beauvoir, for no cause whatever. We say for no cause, as it is obvious that Mr. Kilburn, as the agent of the troupe, could have said nothing against Miss Saville which an outsider, not to say a foreigner like Mr. Beauvoir, had any call to resent. Mr. Kilburn is a gentleman unaccustomed to rough-and-tumble encounters, while his adversary has doubtless associated more with pugilists than gentlemen — at least anyone would think so from his actions yesterday. Beauvoir hustled Mr. Kilburn out of Mr. Mullin's, where the unprovoked assault began, and violently shook him across the new plank sidewalk. The person by the name of Clark, whom Judge Jones for some reason now permits to edit the moribund but once respectable *Gazette*, caught the eye of the congenial Beauvoir, and, true to the ungentlemanly instincts of his base nature, pointed to a barrel in the street. The brutal Englishman took the hint and thrust Mr. Kilburn forcibly into the barrel, leaving the vicinity before Mr. Kilburn, emerging from his close quarters, had fully recovered. What the ruffianly Beauvoir's motive may have been for this wanton assault it is impossible to say; but it is obvious to all why this fellow Clark sought to injure Mr. Kilburn, a gentleman whose many good qualities he of course fails to appreciate. Mr. Kilburn, recognizing the acknowledged merits of our job-office, had given us the contract for all the printing he needed in New Centreville.

Document No. 29.

Advertisement from the New York "Clipper," Dec. 21st, 1878.

WINSTON & MACK'S

GRAND INTERNATIONAL

MEGATHERIUM VARIETY COMBINATION,

COMPANY CALL.

Ladies and Gentlemen of the Company will assemble for rehearsal, at Emerson's Opera House, San Francisco, on Wednesday, Dec. 27th, at 12 M. sharp. Band at 11.   J. B. WINSTON, } Managers.
                                      EDWIN R. MACK, }

Emerson's Opera House,
    San Francisco, Dec. 10th, 1878.
Protean Artist wanted. Would like to hear from Nina Saville.
12—1t*.

Document No. 30.

Letter from Nina Saville to William Beauvoir.

NEW CENTREVILLE, December 26, 1878.

MY DEAR MR. BEAUVOIR—I was very sorry to receive your letter of yesterday — *very* sorry — because there can be only one answer that I can make — and you might well have spared me the pain of saying the word — No. You ask me if I love you. If I did — do you think it would be true love in me to tell you so, when I know what it would cost you? Oh indeed you must never marry *me!* In your own country you would never have heard of me — never seen me — surely never written me such a letter to tell me that you love me and want to marry me. It is not that I am ashamed of my business or of the folks around me, or ashamed that I am only the charity child of two poor players, who lived and died working for the bread for their mouths and mine. I am proud of them — yes, proud of what they did and suffered for one poorer than themselves — a little foundling out of an Indian camp. But I know the difference between you and me. You are a great man at home — you have never told me how great — but I know your father is a rich lord, and I suppose you are. It is not that I think *you* care for that, or think less of me because I was born different from you. I know how good — how kind — how *respectful* you have always been to me — *my lord* — and I shall never forget it — for a girl in my position knows well enough how you might have been otherwise. Oh believe me — *my true friend* — I am never going to forget all you have done for me — and how good it has been to have you near me — a man so different from most others — I don't mean only the kind things you have done — the books and the thoughts and the ways you have taught me to enjoy — and all the trouble you have taken to make me something better than the stupid little girl I was when you found me

— but a great deal more than that — the consideration you have had for me and for what I hold best in the world. I had never met a *gentleman* before — and now the first one I meet — he is my *friend.* That is a great deal.

Only think of it! You have been following me around now for three months, and I have been weak enough to allow it. I am going to do the right thing now. You may think it hard in me *if you really mean what you say,* but even if everything else were right, I would not marry you — because of your rank. I do not know how things are at your home — but something tells me it would be wrong and that your family would have a right to hate you and never forgive you. Professionals cannot go in your society. And that is even if I loved you — and I do not love you — I do not love you — *I do not love you* — now I have written it you will believe it.

So now it is ended — I am going back to the line I was first in — variety — and with a new name. So you can never find me — I entreat you — I beg of you — not to look for me. If you only put your mind to it — you will find it so easy to forget me — for I will not do you the wrong to think that you did not mean what you wrote in your letter or what you said that night *when we sang Annie Laurie together* the last time.   Your sincere friend,

NINA.

Documents Nos. 31 and 32.

Items from San Francisco "Figaro" of December.
29th, 1878:

Nina Saville Co. disbanded New Centreville 26th.
No particulars received.

Winston & Mack's Comb. takes the road December
31st, opening at Tuolumne Hollow. Manager Winston
announces the engagement of Anna Laurie, the Protean
change artiste, with songs, "Don't Get Weary," "Bobbin' Around," "I Yoost Landet."

Document No. 33.

Telegram from Zeke Kilburn, New Centreville, to
Winston and Mack, Emerson's Opera House, San
Francisco, Cal.
NEW CENTREVILLE, Dec. 28, 1878.

Have you vacancy for active and energetic advance
agent. Z. KILBURN.
(9 words 30 paid.)

Document No. 34.

Telegram from Winston and Mack, San Francisco,
to Zeke Kilburn, New Centreville:
SAN FRANCISCO, Dec. 28, 1878.

No.

WINSTON & MACK.
(Collect 30 cents.)

𝔇ocument No. 35.

Bill sent to William Beauvoir, United States Hotel,
Tuolumne Hollow, Cal.:

Tuolumne Hollow, Cal., Dec. 29, 1878.

William Beauvoir, Esq.

Bought of HIMMEL & HATCH,

Opera House Block,

JEWELLERS & DIAMOND MERCHANTS,

Dealers in all kinds of Fancy Goods, Stationery, and Umbrellas, Watches,
Clocks and Barometers.

TERMS CASH.   MUSICAL BOXES REPAIRED.

Dec. 29, *One diamond and enamelled locket* $75.00
   One gold chain 48.00

———
$123.00

Rec'd Payt.

Himmel & Hatch,
per S.

PART FIFTH.

𝔇ocument No. 36.

Letter from Cable J. Dexter, Esq., to Messrs. Pixley
and Sutton, San Francisco.

NEW CENTREVILLE, CAL., March 3, 1879.

Messrs. PIXLEY & SUTTON:

GENTS: I am happy to report that I have at last
reached the bottom level in the case of William Beaver,
alias Beaver Bill, deceased through Indians in 1861.

In accordance with your instructions and check, I proceeded, on the 10th ult., to Shawgum Creek, when I interviewed Blue Horse, chief of the Comanches, who tomahawked subject of your inquiries in the year above mentioned. Found the Horse in the penitentiary, serving out·a drunk and disorderly. Though belligerent at date aforesaid, Horse is now tame, though intemperate. Appeared unwilling to converse, and required stimulants to awaken his memory. Please find enclosed memo. of account for whiskey, covering extra demijohn to corrupt jailer. Horse finally stated that he personally let daylight through deceased, and is willing to guarantee thoroughness of decease. Stated further that aforesaid Beaver's family consisted of squaw and kid. Is willing to swear that squaw was killed, the tribe having no use for her. Killing done by Mule-Who-Goes-Crooked, personal friend of Horse's. The minor child was taken into camp and kept until December of 1863, when tribe dropped to howling cold winter and went on government reservation. Infant (female) was then turned over to U. S. Government at Fort Kearney.

I posted to last-named locality on the 18th ult., and found by the quartermaster's books that, no one appearing to claim the kid, she had been duly indentured, together with six Indians, to a man by the name of Guardine or Sardine (probably the latter), in the show business. The Indians were invoiced as Sage Brush Jimmy, Boiling Hurricane, Mule-Who-Goes-Crooked, Joe, Hairy Grasshopper and Dead Polecat. Child known as White Kitten. Receipt for Indians was signed by Mr. Hi. Samuels, who is still in the circus business, and whom I happen to be selling out at this moment, at suit of McCullum & Montmorency, former partners. Samuels positively identified kid with variety specialist by name of Nina Saville, who has been showing all through this region for a year past.

I shall soon have the pleasure of laying before you documents to establish the complete chain of evidence, from knifing of original subject of your inquiries right up to date.

I have to-day returned from New Centreville, whither I went after Miss Saville. Found she had just skipped the town with a young Englishman by the name of Bovoir, who had been paying her polite attentions for some time, having bowied or otherwise squelched a man for her within a week or two. It appears the young woman had refused to have anything to do with him for a long period; but he seems to have struck pay gravel about two days before my arrival. At present, therefore, the trail is temporarily lost; but I expect to fetch the couple if they are anywhere this side of the Rockies.

Awaiting your further instructions, and cash backing thereto, I am, gents, very resp'y yours,

CABLE J. DEXTER.

Document No. 37.

*Envelope of letter from Sir Oliver Beauvoir, Bart.,
to his son, William Beauvoir.*

Sent to Dead Letter Office

Mr. William Beauvoir

Sherman House Hotel

*Not here
try Brevoort House
N. Y.*   *Chicago*

United States of America

Document No 38.

Letter contained in the envelope above.

CHELSWORTH COTTAGE, March 30, 1879.

MY DEAR BOY: In the sudden blow which has come
upon us all I cannot find words to write. You do not
know what you have done. Your uncle William, after
whom you were named, died in America. He left but
one child, a daughter, the only grandchild of my father
except you. And this daughter is the Miss Nina
Saville with whom you have formed so unhappy a con-
nection. She is your own cousin. She is a Beauvoir.
She is of our blood, as good as any in England.

My feelings are overpowering. I am choked by the
suddenness of this great grief. I cannot write to you
as I would. But I can say this: Do not let me see you
or hear from you until this stain be taken from our name.

OLIVER BEAUVOIR.

Document No. 39.

Cable dispatch of William Beauvoir, Windsor Hotel, New York, to Sir Oliver Beauvoir, Bart., Chelsworth Cottage, Suffolk, England.

NEW YORK, May 1, 1879.

Have posted you Herald.

WILLIAM BEAUVOIR.

Document No. 40.

Advertisement under the head of " Marriages," from the New York " Herald," April 30th, 1879.

BEAUVOIR — BEAUVOIR. — On Wednesday, Jan. 1st, 1879, at Steal Valley, California, by the Rev. Mr. Twells, William Beauvoir, only son of Sir Oliver Beauvoir, of Chelsworth Cottage, Surrey, England, to Nina, only child of the late William Beauvoir, of New Centreville, Cal.

Document No. 41.

Extract from the New York " Herald" of May 29th, 1879.

Among the passengers on the outgoing Cunard steamer *Gallia,* which left New York on Wednesday, was the Honorable William Beauvoir, only son of Sir Oliver Beauvoir, Bart., of England. Mr. Beauvoir has been passing his honeymoon in this city, and, with his charming bride, a famous California belle, has been the recipient of many cordial courtesies from members of our best society. Mr. William Beauvoir is a young man of great promise and brilliant attainments, and is a highly desirable addition to the large and constantly increasing number of aristocratic Britons who seek for wives among the lovely daughters of Columbia. We understand that the bridal pair will take up their residence with the groom's father, at his stately country-seat, Chelsworth Manor, Suffolk.

VENETIAN GLASS.

BY BRANDER MATTHEWS.

I.

IN THE OLD WORLD.

THEY had been to the Lido for a short swim in the slight but bracing surf of the Adriatic. They had had a mid-day breakfast in a queer little restaurant, known only to the initiated, and therefore early discovered by Larry, who had a keen scent for a cook learned in the law. They had loitered along the Riva degli Schiavoni, looking at a perambulatory puppet-show, before which a delighted audience sturdily disregarded the sharp wind which bravely fluttered the picturesque tatters of the spectators; and they were moved to congratulate the Venetians on their freedom from the monotonous repertory of the Anglo-American Punch and Judy, which consists solely of a play really unique in the exact sense of that much-abused word. They were getting their fill of the delicious Italian art which is best described by an American verb — to loaf. And yet they were not wont to be idle, and they had both the sharp, quick American manner, on which laziness sits uneasily and infrequently.

48

John Manning and Laurence Laughton were both young New Yorkers. Larry — for so in youth was he called by everybody pending the arrival of years which should make him a universal uncle, to be known of all men as "Uncle Larry" — was as pleasant a travelling companion as one could wish. He was the only son and heir of a father, now no more, but vaguely understood when alive and in the flesh to have been "in the China trade;" although whether this meant crockery or Cathay no one was able with precision to declare. Larry Laughton had been graduated from Columbia College with the class of 1860, and the following spring found him here in Venice after a six months' ramble through Europe with his old friend, John Manning, partly on foot and partly in an old carriage of their own, in which they enjoyed the fast-vanishing pleasures of posting.

John Manning was a little older than Larry; he had left West Point in 1854 with a commission as second lieutenant in the Old Dragoons. For nearly six years he did his duty in that state of life in which it pleased the Secretary of War and General Scott to call him; he had crossed the plains one bleak winter to a post in the Rocky Mountains, and he had danced through two summers at Fort Adams at Newport; he had been stationed for a while in New Mexico, where there was an abundance of the pleasant sport of Indian-fighting, — even now he had only to make believe a little to see the tufted head of a Navajo peer around the columns supporting the Lion of Saint Mark, or to mistake the fringe of *facchini* on the edge of the Grand Canal for a group of the shiftless half-breeds of New Mexico. In time the Old Dragoons had been ordered North, where the work was then less pleasant than on the border; and, in fact, it was a distinct unwillingness to execute the Fugitive Slave Law which forced John Manning to resign his commission in the army, although it was the hanging of John Brown which drew from him the actual letter of resignation. Before settling down to other work — for he was a man who could not and would not be idle — he had gratified his long desire of taking a turn through the Old World. Larry Laughton had joined him in Holland, where he had been making researches into the family history, and proving to his own satisfaction at least that the New York Mannings, in spite of their English name, had come from Amsterdam to New Amsterdam. And now, toward the end of April, 1861, John Manning and Laurence Laughton stood on the Rialto, hesitating *Fra Marco e Todaro*, as the Venetians have it, in uninterested question whether they should go into the Ghetto, among the hideous homes of the chosen people, or out again to Murano for a second visit to the famous factory of Venetian glass.

"I say, John," remarked Larry as they lazily debated the question, gazing meanwhile on the steady succession of gondolas coming and going to and from the steps by the side of the bridge, "I'd as lief, if not liefer, go to Murano again, if they've any of their patent anti-poison goblets left. You know they say they used to make a glass so fine that it was shattered into shivers whenever poison might be poured into it. Of course I don't believe it, but a glass like that would be mighty handy in the sample-rooms of New York. I'm afraid a man walking up Broadway could use up a gross of the anti-poison goblets before he got one straight drink of the genuine article, unadulterated and drawn from the wood."

"You must not make fun of a poetic legend, Larry. You have to believe everything over here, or you do not get the worth of your money," said John Manning.

"Well, I don't know," was Larry's reply; "I don't know just what to believe. I was talking about it last night at Florian's, while you were writing letters home."

"I did not know Mr. Laughton had friends in Venice."

"Oh, I can make friends anywhere. And this one was lots of fun. He was a priest, an *abbate*, I think he calls himself. He had read five newspapers in the *caffè* and paid for one tiny cup of coffee. When I finished the *Débats* I passed it to him for his sixth — and he spoke to me in French, and I wasn't going to let an Italian talk French to me without answering back, so I just sailed in and began to swap stories with him."

"No doubt you gave him much valuable information."

"Well, I did; I just exuded information. Why the first thing he said, when I told him I was an American, was to wonder whether I hadn't met his brother, who was also in America — in Rio Janeiro — just as if Rio was the other side of the North River."

John Manning smiled at Larry's disgusted expression, and asked, "What has this *abbate* to do with the fragile Venetian glass?"

"Only this," answered Larry. "I told him two or three Northwesters, just as well as I could in French, and then he said that marvellous things were also done here once upon a time. And he told me about the glass which broke when poison was poured into it."

"It is a pleasant superstition," said John Manning. "I think Poe makes use of it, and I believe Shakespeare refers to it."

"But did either Poe or Shakespeare say anything about the two goblets just alike, made for the twin brothers Manin nearly four hundred years ago? Did they tell you how one glass was shivered by poison and its owner killed, and how the other brother had to flee for his life? Did they inform you that the unbroken goblet exists to this day, and is in fact now for sale by an Hebrew Jew who peddles antiquities? Did they tell you that?"

"Neither Edgar Allan Poe nor William Shakespeare ever disturbs my slumbers by telling me anything of the sort," laughed Manning.

"Well, my *abbate* told me just that, and he gave me the address of the Shylock who has the surviving goblet for sale."

"Suppose we go there and see it," suggested Manning, "and you can tell me the whole story of the twin brothers as we go along."

"Shall we take a gondola or walk?" was Larry's interrogative acceptance of the suggestion.

"It's in the Ghetto, isn't it?"

"Most of the Jew curiosity dealers have left the Ghetto. Our Shylock has a palace on the Grand Canal.

I guess we had better take a gondola, though it can't
be far."

So they sat themselves down in one of the aquatic
cabs which ply the water streets of the city in the sea.
The gondolier stood to his oar and put his best foot
foremost, and as the boat sped forward on its way along
the great S of the Grand Canal, Larry told the tale of
the twin brothers and the shattered goblet.

" Well, it seems that some time in the sixteenth century, say three hundred years ago or thereabout, there
were several branches of the great and powerful Manin
family — the same family to which the patriotic Daniele
Manin belonged, you know. And at the head of one
of these branches were the twin brothers Marco Manin
and Giovanni Manin. Now, these brothers were devoted to each other, and they had only one thought,
one word, one deed. When one of them happened to
think of a thing, it often happened that the other
brother did it. So it was not surprising that they both
fell in love with the same woman. She was a danger-
ous-looking, yellow-haired woman, with steel-gray eyes
— that is, if her eyes were not really green, as to which
there was doubt. But there was no doubt at all that
she was powerfully handsome. The *abbate* said that
there was a famous portrait of her in one of these
churches as a Saint Mary Magdalen, with her hair
down. She was a splendid creature, and lots of men
were running after her besides the twin Manins. The
two brothers did not quarrel with each other about the
woman, but they did quarrel with some of her other
lovers, and particularly with a nobleman of the highest

rank and power, who was supposed to belong not only to the Council of Ten, but to the Three. Between this man and the Manins there was war to the knife and the knife to the hilt. One day Marco Manin expressed a wish for one of these goblets of Venetian glass so fine that poison shatters it, and so Giovanni went out to Murano and ordered two of them, of the very finest quality, and just alike in every particular of color and shape and size. You see the twins always had everything in pairs. But the people at Murano somehow misunderstood the order, and although they made both glasses they sent home only one. Marco Manin was at table when it arrived, and he took it in his hand at once, and after admiring its exquisite workmanship — you see, all these old Venetians had the art-feeling strongly developed — he told a servant to fill it to the brim with Cyprus wine. But as he raised the flowing cup to his lips it shivered in his grasp and the wine was spilt on the marble floor. He drew his sword and slew the servant who had sought to betray him, and rushing into the street he found himself face to face with the enemy whom he knew to have instigated the attempt. They crossed swords at once, but, before Marco Manin could have a fair fight for his life, he was stabbed in the back by a glass stiletto, the hilt of which was broken off short in the wound."

"Where was his brother all this time?" was the first question with which John Manning broke the thread of his friend's story.

"He had been to see the yellow-haired beauty, and he came back just in time to meet his brother's lifeless body as it was carried into their desolate home. Holding his dead brother's hand, as he had often held it living, he promised his brother to avenge his death without delay and at any cost. Then he prepared at once for flight. He knew that Venice would be too hot to hold him when the deed was done; and besides, he felt that without his brother life in Venice would be intolerable. So he made ready for flight. Twenty-four hours to a minute after Marco Manin's death the body of the hireling assassin was sinking to the bottom of the Grand Canal, while the man who had paid for the murder lay dead on the same spot with the point of a glass stiletto in his heart! And when they wanted to send him the other goblet, there was no one to send it to: Giovanni Manin had disappeared."

"Where had he gone?" queried John Manning.

"That's what I asked the *abbate*, and he said he did n't know for sure, but that in those days Venice had a sizable trade with the Low Countries, and there was a tradition that Giovanni Manin had gone to the Netherlands."

"To Holland?" asked John Manning with unwonted interest.

"Yes, to Amsterdam, or to Rotterdam, or to some one of those -dam towns, as we used to call them in our geography class."

"It was to Amsterdam," said Manning, speaking as one who had certain information.

"How do you know that?" asked Larry. "Even the *abbate* said it was only a tradition that he had gone to Holland at all."

"He went to Amsterdam," said Manning; "that I know."

Before Larry could ask how it was that his friend knew anything about the place of exile of a man whom he had never heard of ten minutes earlier, the gondola had paused before the door of the palace in which dwelt the dealer in antiquities who had in his possession the famous goblet of Venetian glass. As they ascended to the sequence of rambling rooms cluttered with old furniture, rusty armor, and odds and ends of statuary, in which the modern Jew of Venice sat at the receipt of custom, both Larry Laughton and John Manning had to give their undivided attention to the framing in Italian of their wishes. Shylock himself was a venerable and benevolent person, with a look of wonderful shrewdness and an incomprehensibility of speech, for he spoke the Venetian dialect with a harsh Jewish accent, either of which would have daunted a linguistic veteran. Plainly enough, conversation was impossible, for he could barely understand their American-Italian, and they could not at all understand his Jewish-Venetian. But it would not do to let these *Inglesi* go away without paying tribute.

" *Ciò!* " said Shylock, smiling graciously at his futile attempts to open communication with the enemy. Then he called Jessica from the deep window where she had been at work on the quaint old account-books of the shop, as great curiosities as anything in it, since they were kept in Venetian, but by means of the Hebrew alphabet. She spoke Italian, and to her the young men made known their wants.

She said a few words to her father, and he brought forth the goblet.

It was a marvellous specimen of the most exquisite Venetian workmanship. A pair of green serpents, with eyes that glowed like fire, writhed around the golden stem of a blood-red bowl, and as the white light of the cloudless sky fell on it from the broad window, it burned in the glory of the sunshine and seemed to fill itself full of some mysterious and royal wine. Shylock revolved it slowly in his hand to show the strange waviness of its texture, and as it turned, the serpents clung more closely to the stem and arched their heads and shot a glance of hate at the strangers who came to gaze on them with curious fascination.

John Manning looked at the goblet long and eagerly. "How did it come into your possession?" he asked.

And Jessica translated Shylock's declaration that the goblet had been at Murano for hundreds of years; it was *anticho — antichissimo,* as the signor could see for himself. It was of the best period of the art. That Shylock would guarantee. How came it into his possession? By the greatest good fortune. It was taken from Murano during the troubles after the fall of the Republic in the time of Napoleon. It had gone finally into the hands of a certain count, who, very luckily, was poor. *Conte che non conta, non conta niente.* So Shylock had been enabled to buy it. It had been the desire of his heart for years to own so fine an object.

"How much do you want for it?" asked John Manning.

Shylock scented from afar the battle of bargaining, dear in Italy to both buyer and seller. He gave a keen look at both the *Inglesi,* and took up the glass affectionately, as though he could not bear to part with it. Jessica interpreted. Shylock had intended that goblet for his own private collection, but the frank and generous manner of their excellencies had overcome him, and he would let them have it for five hundred florins.

"Five hundred florins! Phew!" whistled Larry, astonished in spite of his initiation into the mysteries of Italian bargaining. "Well, if you were to ask me the Shakespearian conundrum, Hath not a Jew eyes? I shouldn't give it up; I should say he has eyes — for the main chance."

"Five hundred florins," said John Manning. "Very well. I'll take it."

Shylock's astonishment at getting four times what he would have taken was equalled only by his regret that he had not asked twice as much.

"Can you pack it so that I can take it to New York safely?"

"*Sicuro, signor,*" and Shylock agreed to have the precious object boxed with all possible care and despatch, and delivered at the hotel that afternoon.

"*Servo suo!*" said Jessica, as they stood at the door.

"*Bon di, Patron!*" responded Larry, in Venetian fashion; then as the door closed behind them he said to John Manning, "Seems to me you were in a hurry! You could have had that glass for half the money."

"Perhaps I could," was Manning's quiet reply, "but I was eager to get it back at once."

"Get it back? Why, it was n't stolen from *you*, was it? I never did suppose *he* came by it honestly."

"It was not stolen from me personally, but it belonged to my family. It was made for Giovanni Manin, who fled from Venice to Amsterdam three hundred odd years ago. His grandson and namesake left Amsterdam for New Amsterdam half a century later. And when the English changed New Amsterdam into New York, Jan Mannin became John Manning — and I am his direct descendant, and the first of my blood to return to Venice to get the goblet Giovanni Manin ordered and left behind."

"Well, I 'm damned!" said Larry, pensively.

"And now," continued John Manning as they took their seats in the gondola, "tell the man to go to the church where the picture of Mary Magdalen is. I want a good look at that woman!"

In the evening, as John Manning sat in a little *caffè* under the arcades of the Piazza San Marco, sipping a tiny cup of black coffee, Larry entered with a rush of righteous indignation.

"What 's the matter, Larry?" was John Manning's calm query.

"There 's the devil to pay at home. South Carolina has fired on the flag at Sumter."

Three weeks later Colonel Manning was assigned to duty drilling the raw recruits soon to be the Army of the Potomac.

II.

IN THE NEW WORLD.

In the month of February, 1864, a chance newspaper paragraph informed whom it might concern that Major Laurence Laughton, having three weeks' leave of absence from his regiment, was at the Astor House. In consequence of this advertisement of his whereabouts, Major Laughton received many cheerful circulars and letters, in most of which his attention was claimed for the artificial limb made by the advertiser. He also received a letter from Colonel John Manning, urgently bidding him to come out for a day at least to his little place on the Hudson, where he was lying sick, and, as he feared, sick unto death. On the receipt of this Larry cut short a promising flirtation with a war-widow who sat next him at table, and took the first train up the river. It was a bleak day, and there was at least a foot of snow on the ground, as hard and as dry as though it had clean forgot that it was made of water. As Larry left the little station, to which the train had slowly struggled at last, an hour behind time, the wind sprang up again and began to moan around his feet and to sting his face with icy shot; and as he trudged across the desolate path which led to Manning's lonely house he discovered that rude Boreas could be as keen a sharp-shooter as any in the rifle-pits around Richmond. A hard walk up-hill for a quarter of an hour brought him to the brow of the cliff on which stood the forlorn and wind-swept house where John Manning lay. An unkempt and hideous old crone as black as night opened the door for him. He left in the hall his hat and overcoat and a little square box he had brought in his hand; and then he followed the ebony hag upstairs to Colonel Manning's room. Here at the door she left him, after giving a sharp knock. A weak voice said, "Come in!"

Laurence Laughton entered the room with a quick step, but the light-hearted words with which he had meant to encourage his friend died on his lips as soon as he saw how grievously that friend had changed. John Manning had faded to a shadow of his former self; the light of his eye was quenched, and the spirit within him seemed broken; the fine, sensitive, noble face lay white against the pillow, looking weary and wan and hopeless. The effort to greet his friend exhausted him and brought on a hard cough, and he pressed his hand to his breast as though some hidden malady were gnawing and burning within.

"Well, John," said Larry, as he took a seat by the bedside, "why didn't you let me know before now that you were laid up? I could have got away a month ago."

"Time enough yet," said John Manning slowly; "time enough yet. I shall not die for another week, I fear."

"Why, man, you must not talk like that. You are as good as a dozen dead men yet," said Larry, trying to look as cheerful as might be.

"I am as good as dead myself," said his friend

seriously, as befitted a man under the shadow of death; "and I have no wish to live. The sooner I am out of this pain and powerlessness the better I shall like it."

"I say, John, old man, this is no way for you to talk! Brace up, and you will soon be another man!"

"I shall soon be in another world, I hope," and the helpless misery of the tone in which these few words were said smote Laurence Laughton to the heart.

"What's the matter with you?" he asked with as lively an air as he could attain, for the ominous and inexplicable sadness of the situation was fast taking hold on him.

"I have a bullet through the lungs and a pain in the heart."

"But men do not die of a bullet in the lungs and a pain in the heart," was Larry's encouraging response.

"I shall."

"Why should you more than others?"

"Because there is something else — something mysterious, some unknown malady — which bears me down and burns me up. There is no use trying to deceive me, Larry. My papers are made out, and I shall get my discharge from the Army of the Living in a very few days now. But I must not waste the little breath I have left in talking about myself. I sent for you to ask a favor."

Larry held out his hand, and John Manning took it, and seemed to gain strength from the firm clasp.

"I knew I could rely on you," he said, "for much or for little. And this is not much, for I have not much to leave. This worn old house, which belonged to my grandmother, and in which I spent the happiest hours of my boyhood, this and a few shares of stock here and there are all I have to leave. I do not know what the house is worth, and I shall be glad when I am gone from it. If I had not come here, I think I might perhaps have got well. There seems to be something deadly about the place." The sick man's voice sank to a wavering whisper, as if it were borne down by a sudden weight of impending danger against which he might struggle in vain; he gave a fearful glance about the room, as though seeking a mystic foe, hidden and unknown. "The very first day we were here the cat lapped its milk by the fire and then stretched itself out and died without a sign. And I had not been here two days before I felt the fatal influence: the trouble from my wound came on again, and this awful burning in my breast began to torture me. As a boy, I thought that heaven must be like this house; and now I should not want to die if I thought hell could be worse!"

"Why don't you leave the hole, since you hate it so?" asked Larry, with what scant cheeriness he could muster; he was yielding himself slowly to the place, though he fought bravely against his superstitious weakness.

"Am I fit to be moved?" was Manning's query in reply.

"But you will be better soon, and then"—

"I shall be worse before I am better, and I shall never be better in this life or in this place. No, no, I must die in my hole, like a dog. Like a dog!" and

John Manning repeated the words with a wistful face.
"Do you remember the faithful beast who always
welcomed me here when we came up before we went
to Europe?"

"Of course I do," said Larry, glad to get the sick
man away from his sickness, and to ease his mind by
talk on a healthy topic; "he was a splendid fellow, too.
Cæsar, that was his name, wasn't it?"

"Cæsar Borgia I called him," was Manning's sad
reply. "I knew you could not have forgotten him.
He is dead. Cæsar Borgia is dead. He was the last
living thing that loved me — except you, Larry, I know
— and he is dead. He died this morning. He came
to my bedside as usual, and he licked my hand gently
and looked up in my face, and laid him down along-
side of me on the carpet here and died. Poor Cæsar
Borgia — he loved me, and he is dead! And you,
Larry, you must not stay here. The air is fatal.
Every breath may be your last. When you have heard
what I want, you must be off at once. If you like, you
may come up again to the funeral before your leave is
up. I saw you had three weeks."

Laurence Laughton moved uneasily in his chair and
swallowed with difficulty. "John," he managed to
say after an effort, "if you talk to me like that, I shall
go at once. Tell me what it is you want me to do for
you."

"I want you to take care of my wife and of my
child, if there be one born to me after my death."

"Your wife?" repeated Larry, in staring surprise.

"You did not know I was married? I knew it at

the time, as the boy said," and John Manning smiled
bitterly.

"Where is she?" was Larry's second query.

"Here."

"Here?"

"In this house. You shall see her before you go.
And after the funeral I want you to get her away from
here with what speed you can. Sell this house for
what it will bring, and put the money into government
bonds. You may find it hard to persuade her to
move, for she seems to have a strange liking for this
place. She breathes freely in the deadly air that suf-
focates me. But you must not let her remain here;
this is no place for her now that a new life and new
duties are before her."

"How was it I did not know of your marriage?"
asked Larry.

"I knew nothing about it myself twenty-four hours
before it happened," answered John Manning. "You
need not look surprised. It is a simple story. I had
this shot through the breast at Gettysburg last Fourth
of July. I lay on the hillside a day and a night before
relief came. Then a farmer took me into his house.
A military surgeon dressed my wounds, but I owed
my life to the nursing and care and unceasing attention
of a young lady who was staying with the farmer's
daughter. She had been doing her duty as a nurse
as near to the field as she could go ever since the first
Bull Run. She saved my life, and I gave it to her —
what there was of it. She was a beautiful woman,
indeed I never saw a more beautiful — and she has a

strange likeness to — but that you shall see for yourself when you see her. She is getting a little rest now, for she has been up all night attending to me. She *will* wait on me in spite of all I say; of course I know there is no use wasting effort on me now. She is the most devoted nurse in the world; and we shall part as we met — she taking care of me at the last as she did at the first. Would God our relation had never been other than patient and nurse! It would have been better for both had we never been husband and wife!" And John Manning turned his face to the wall with a weary sigh; then he coughed harshly, and raised his hand to his breast as though to stifle the burning within him.

"It seems to me, John, that you ought not to talk like that of the woman you loved," said Laurence Laughton, with unusual seriousness.

"I never loved her," answered Manning, coldly. Then he turned, and asked hastily, "Do you think I should want to die if I loved her?"

"But she loves you," said Laurence.

"She never loved me!" was Manning's impatient retort.

"Then why were you married?"

"That's what I would like to know. It was fate, I suppose. What is to be, is. I never used to believe in predestination, but I know that of my own free will I could never have done what I did."

"I confess I do not understand you," said Larry.

"I do not understand myself. There is so much in this world that is mysterious — I hope the next will be different. I was under the charm, I fancy, when I married her. She is a beautiful woman, as I told you, and I was a man, and I was weak, and I had hope. Why she married me that early September evening I do not know. It was not long before we both found out our mistake. And it was too late then. We were man and wife. Don't suppose I blame her — I do not. I have no cause of complaint. She is a good wife to me, as I have tried to be a good husband to her. We made a mistake in marrying each other, and we know it — that's all!"

Before Laurence Laughton could answer, the door opened gently and Mrs. Manning entered the room. Laurence rose to greet his friend's wife, but the act was none the less a homage to her resplendent beauty. In spite of the worn look of her face, she was the most beautiful woman he had ever seen. She had tawny, tigress hair, and hungry, tigress eyes. The eyes, indeed, were fathomless and indescribable, and their fitful glance had something uncanny about it. The hair was nearly of the true Venetian color, and she had the true Venetian sumptuousness of appearance, simple as was her attire. She seemed as though she had just risen from the couch whereon she reclined before Titian or Tintoretto, and, having clothed herself, had walked forth in this nineteenth century and these United States. She was a strange and striking figure, and Laurence found it impossible to analyze exactly the curious and weird impression she produced on him. Her voice, as she greeted him, gave him a peculiar thrill; and when he shook hands with her he seemed to feel himself face to face with some strange being from another land and another century. She inspired him with a supernatural awe he was not wont to feel in the presence of woman. He had a dim consciousness that there lingered in his memory the glimmering image of some woman seen somewhere, he knew not when, who was like unto the woman before him.

As she took her seat by the side of the bed she gave Laurence Laughton a look that seemed to peer into his soul. Laurence felt himself quiver under it. It was a look to make a man fearful. Then John Manning, who had moved uneasily as his wife entered, said, "Laurence, can you see any resemblance in my wife to any one you ever saw before?"

Their eyes met again, and again Laurence had a vague remembrance as though he and she had stood face to face before in some earlier existence. Then his wandering recollections took shape, and he remembered the face and the form and the haunting mystery of the expression, and he felt for a moment as though he had been permitted to peer into the cabalistic darkness of an awful mystery, though he failed wholly to perceive its occult significance — if significance there were of any sort.

"I think I do remember," he said at last. "It was in Venice — at the Church of Santa Maria Magdalena — the picture there that " —

"You remember aright!" interrupted John Manning. "My wife is the living image of the Venetian woman for whose beauty Marco Manin was one day

stabbed in the back with a glass stiletto, and Giovanni
Manin fled from the place of his birth and never saw it
again. It is idle to fight against the stars in their
courses. We met here in the New World, she and I,
as they met in the Old World so long ago — and the
end is the same. It was to be — it was to be!"

Laurence Laughton gave a swift glance at his friend's
wife to see what effect these words might have on her,
and he was startled to detect on her face the same
enigmatic smile which was the chief memory he had
retained of the Venetian picture. Truly the likeness
between the painting and the wife of his friend was
marvellous; and Laurence tried to shake off a morbid
wonder whether there might be any obscure and inscrutable survival from one generation to another across
the seas and across the years.

"If you remember the picture," said John Manning,
"perhaps you remember the quaint goblet of Venetian
glass I bought the same day?"

"Of course I do," said Larry, glad to get Manning
started on a topic of talk a little less personal.

"Perhaps you know what has become of it?" asked
Manning.

"I can answer 'of course' to that, too," replied
Larry, "because I have it here."

"Here?"

"Here — in a little square box, in the hall," answered
Larry. "I had it in my trunk, you know, when we
took passage on the *Vanderbilt* at Havre that May
morning. I forgot to give it to you in the hurry of
landing, and I haven't had a chance since. This is the

first time I have seen you for nearly three years. I found the box this morning, and I thought you might like to have it again, so I brought it up."

John Manning rang the bell at the head of his bed. The black crone answered it, and soon returned with the little square box. Manning impatiently broke the seals and cords that bound its cover and began eagerly to release the goblet from the cotton and tissue paper in which it had been carefully swathed and bandaged. Mrs. Manning, though her moods were subtler and more intense, showed an anxiety to see the goblet quite as feverish as her husband's. In a minute the last wrapping was twisted off and the full beauty of the Venetian glass was revealed to them. Assuredly no praise was too loud for its delicate and exquisite workmanship.

"Does Mrs. Manning know the story of the goblet?" asked Larry; "has she been told of the peculiar virtue ascribed to it?"

"She has too great a fondness for the horrible and the fantastic not to have heard the story in its smallest details," said Manning.

Mrs. Manning had taken the glass in her fine, thin hands. Evidently it and its mystic legend had a morbid fascination for her. A strange light gleamed in her wondrous eyes, and Laughton was startled again to see the extraordinary resemblance between her and the picture they had looked at on the day the goblet had been bought.

"When the poison was poured into it," she said at last, with quick and restless glances at the two men, "the glass broke — then the tale was true?"

" It was a coincidence only, I 'm afraid," said her husband, who had rallied and regained strength under the unwonted excitement.

Just then the old-fashioned clock on the stairs struck five. Mrs. Manning started up, holding the goblet in her hand.

" It is time for your medicine," she said.

" As you please," answered her husband wearily, sinking back on his pillow. " My wife insists on giving me every drop of my potions with her own hands. I shall not trouble her much longer, and I doubt if it is any use for her to trouble me now."

" I shall give you everything in this glass after this," she said.

" In the Venetian glass?" asked Larry.

" Yes," she said, turning on him fiercely; " why not?"

" Do you think the doctor is trying to poison me?" asked her husband.

" No, I do not think the doctor is trying to poison you," she repeated mechanically, as she moved toward a little sideboard in a corner of the room. " But I shall give you all your medicines in this hereafter."

She stood at the little sideboard, with her back toward them, and she mingled the contents of various phials in the Venetian goblet. Then she turned to cross the room to her husband. As she walked with the glass in her hand there was a rift in the clouds high over the other side of the river, and the rays of the setting sun thrust themselves through the window and lighted up the glory of her hair and showed the strange

gleam in her staring eyes.   Another step, and the red
rays fell on the Venetian glass, and it burned and
glowed, and the green serpents twined about its ruby
stem seemed to twist and crawl with malignant life,
while their scorching eyes shot fire.   Another step, and
she stood by the bedside.   As John Manning reached
out his hand for the goblet, a tremor passed through
her, her fingers clinched the fragile stem, and the glass
fell on the floor and was shattered to shivers as its
fellow had been shattered three centuries ago and more.
She still stared steadily before her; then her lips parted,
and she said, "The glass broke — the glass broke —
then the tale is true!"   And with one hysteric shriek
she fell forward amid the fragments of the Venetian
goblet, unconscious thereafter of all things.

THE RED SILK HANDKERCHIEF.

BY H. C. BUNNER.

THE yellow afternoon sun came in through the long
blank windows of the room wherein the Superior
Court of the State of New York, Part II., Gillespie,
Judge, was·in session. The hour of adjournment was
near at hand, a dozen court-loungers slouched on the
hard benches in the attitudes of cramped carelessness
which mark the familiar of the halls of justice. Beyond the rail sat a dozen lawyers and lawyers' clerks,
and a dozen weary jurymen. Above the drowsy
silence rose the nasal voice of the junior counsel for
the defence, who in a high monotone, with his faint
eyes fixed on the paper in his hand, was making something like a half-a-score of "requests to charge."

Nobody paid attention to him. Two lawyers' clerks
whispered like mischievous schoolboys, hiding behind
a pile of books that towered upon a table. Junior
counsel for the plaintiff chewed his pencil and took
advantage of his opportunity to familiarize himself
with certain neglected passages of the New Code.
The crier, like a half-dormant old spider, sat in his
place and watched a boy who was fidgetting at the far
end of the room, and who looked as though he wanted
to whistle.

73

The jurymen might have been dream-men, vague creations of an autumn afternoon's doze. It was hard to connect them with a world of life and business. Yet, gazing closer, you might have seen that one looked as if he were thinking of his dinner, and another as if he were thinking of the lost love of his youth ; and that the expression on the faces of the others ranged from the vacant to the inscrutable. The oldest juror, at the end of the second row, was sound asleep. Everyone in the court-room, except himself, knew it. No one cared.

Gillespie, J., was writing his acceptance of an invitation to a dinner set for that evening at Delmonico's. He was doing this in such a way that he appeared to be taking copious and conscientious notes. Long years on the bench had whitened Judge Gillespie's hair, and taught him how to do this. His seeming attentiveness much encouraged the counsel for the defence, whose high-pitched tone rasped the air like the buzzing of a bee that has found its way through the slats of the blind into some darkened room, of a summer noon, and that, as it seeks angrily for egress, raises its shrill scandalized protest against the idleness and the pleasant gloom.

"We r'quest y'r Honor t' charge: First, 't forcible entry does not const'oot tresp'ss, 'nless intent's proved. Thus, 'f a man rolls down a bank"—

But the judge's thoughts were in the private supper-room at Delmonico's. He had no interest in the sad fate of the hero of the supposititious case, who had been obliged, by a strange and ingenious combination of accidents, to make violent entrance, incidentally damaging the persons and property of others, into the lands and tenements of his neighbor.

And further away yet the droning lawyer had set a-travelling the thoughts of Horace Walpole, clerk for Messrs. Weeden, Snowden & Gilfeather; for the young man sat with his elbows on the table, his head in his hands, a sad half-smile on his lips, and his brown eyes looking through vacancy to St. Lawrence County, New York.

He saw a great, shabby old house, shabby with the awful shabbiness of a sham grandeur laid bare by time and mocked of the pitiless weather. There was a great sham Grecian portico at one end; the white paint was well-nigh washed away, and the rain-streaked wooden pillars seemed to be weeping tears of penitence for having lied about themselves and pretended to be marble.

The battened walls were cracked and blistered. The Grecian temple on the hillock near looked much like a tomb, and not at all like a summer-house. The flower-garden was so rank and ragged, so overgrown with weed and vine, that it was spared the mortification of revealing its neglected maze, the wonder of the county in 1820. All was sham, save the decay. That was real; and by virtue of its decrepitude the old house seemed to protest against modern contempt, as though it said: "I have had my day. I was built when people thought this sort of thing was the right sort of thing; when we had our own little pseudo-classic renaissance in America. I lie between the towns of Aristotle and Sabine Farms. I am a gen-

tleman's residence, and my name is Montevista. I was
built by a prominent citizen. You need not laugh
through your lattices, you smug new Queen Anne cottage, down there in the valley! What will become of
you when the falsehood is found out of your imitation
bricks and your tiled roof of shingles, and your stained
glass that is only a sheet of transparent paper pasted
on a pane? You are a young sham; I am an old one.
Have some respect for age!"

Its age was the crowning glory of the estate of
Montevista. There was nothing new on the place
except a third mortgage. Yet had Montevista villa
put forth a juster claim to respect, it would have said:
"I have had my day. Where all is desolate and silent
now, there was once light and life. Along these halls
and corridors, the arteries of my being, pulsed a hot
blood of joyous humanity, fed with delicate fare, kin-
dled with generous wine. Every corner under my roof
was alive with love and hope and ambition. Great
men and dear women were here; and the host was
great and the hostess was gracious among them all.
The laughter of children thrilled my gaudily decked
stucco. To-day an old man walks up and down my
lonely drawing-rooms, with bent head, murmuring to
himself odds and ends of tawdry old eloquence, wandering in a dead land of memory, waiting till Death
shall take him by the hand and lead him out of his
ruinous house, out of his ruinous life."

Death had indeed come between Horace and the
creation of his spiritual vision. Never again should
the old man walk, as to the boy's eyes he walked now,

over the creaking floors, from where the Nine Muses
simpered on the walls of the south parlor to where
Homer and Plutarch, equally simpering, yet simpering
with a difference,—severely simpering,—faced each
other across the north room. Horace saw his father
stalking on his accustomed round, a sad, familiar figure,
tall and bent. The hands were clasped behind the
back, the chin was bowed on the black stock; but every
now and then the thin form drew itself straight, the
fine, clean-shaven, aquiline face was raised, beaming
with the ghost of an old enthusiasm, and the long right
arm was lifted high in the air as he began, his sonorous
tones a little tremulous in spite of the restraint of old-
time pomposity and deliberation,—

"Mr. Speaker, I rise;"—or, "If your Honor
please "—

The forlorn, helpless earnestness of this mockery of
life touched Horace's heart; and yet he smiled to think
how different were the methods and manners of his
father from those of brother Hooper, whose requests
still droned up to the reverberating hollows of the roof,
and there were lost in a subdued boom and snarl of
echoes such as a court-room only can beget.

Two generations ago, when the Honorable Horace
Kortlandt Walpole was the rising young lawyer of the
State; when he was known as "the Golden-Mouthed
Orator of St. Lawrence County," he was in the habit
of assuming that he owned whatever court he practised
in; and, as a rule, he was right. The most bullock-
brained of country judges deferred to the brilliant
young master of law and eloquence, and his "requests"

were generally accepted as commands and obeyed as
such. Of course the great lawyer, for form's sake, threw
a veil of humility over his deliverances; but even that
he rent to shreds when the fire of his eloquence once
got fairly aglow.

"May it please your Honor! Before your Honor
exercises the sacred prerogative of your office — before
your Honor performs the sacred duty which the State
has given into your hands — before, with that lucid
genius to which I bow my head, you direct the minds
of these twelve good men and true in the path of strict
judicial investigation, I ask your Honor to instruct them
that they must bring to their deliberations that im-
partial justice which the laws of our beloved country
— of which no abler exponent than your Honor has
ever graced the bench, — which the laws of our beloved
country guarantee to the lowest as well as to the
loftiest of her citizens — from the President in the
Executive Mansion to the humble artisan at the forge
— throughout this broad land, from the lagoons of
Louisiana to where the snow-clad forests of Maine hurl
defiance at the descendants of Tory refugees in the
barren wastes of Nova Scotia " —

Horace remembered every word and every gesture
of that speech. He recalled even the quick upward
glance from under the shaggy eyebrows with which
his father seemed to see again the smirking judge
catching at the gross bait of flattery; he knew the
little pause which the speaker's memory had filled with
the applause of an audience long since dispersed to
various silent country graveyards; and he wondered,

pityingly, if it were possible that even in his father's prime that wretched allusion to old political hatreds had power to stir the fire of patriotism in the citizen's bosom.

"Poor old father!" said the boy to himself. The voice which had for so many years been but an echo was stilled wholly now. Brief victory and long defeat were nothing now to the golden-mouthed orator.

"Shall I fail as he failed?" thought Horace: "No! I can't. Haven't I got *her* to work for?"

And then he drew out of his breast pocket a red silk handkerchief and turned it over in his hand with a movement that concealed and caressed at the same time.

It was a very red handkerchief. It was not vermilion, nor "cardinal," nor carmine, — a strange Oriental idealization of blood-red which lay well on the soft, fine, luxurious fabric. But it was an unmistakable, a shameless, a barbaric red.

And as he looked at it, young Hitchcock, of Hitchcock & Van Rensselaer, came up behind him and leaned over his shoulder.

"Where did you get the handkerchief, Walpole?" he whispered; "you ought to hang that out for an auction flag, and sell out your cases."

Horace stuffed it back in his pocket.

"You'd be glad enough to buy some of them, if you got the show," he returned; but the opportunity for a prolonged contest of wit was cut short. The judge was folding his letter, and the nasal counsel, having finished his reading, stood gazing in doubt and trepi-

dation at the bench, and asking himself why his Honor
had not passed on each point as presented. He found
out.

"Are you prepared to submit those requests in
writing?" demanded Gillespie, J., sharply and suddenly. He knew well enough that that poor little
nasal, nervous junior counsel would never have trusted
himself to speak ten consecutive sentences in court
without having every word on paper before him.

"Ye-yes," the counsel stammered, and handed up
his careful manuscript.

"I will examine these to-night," said his Honor, and,
apparently, he made an endorsement on the papers.
He was really writing the address on the envelope of
his letter. Then there was a stir, and a conversation
between the judge and two or three lawyers, all at
once, which was stopped when his Honor gave an
Olympian nod to the clerk.

The crier arose.

"He' ye! he' ye! he' ye!" he shouted with perfunc-
tory vigor. "Wah—wah—wah!" the high ceiling
slapped back at him; and he declaimed, on one note,
a brief address to "Awperns han bins" in that court,
of which nothing was comprehensible save the words
"Monday next at eleven o'clock." And then the
court collectively rose, and individually put on hats for
the most part of the sort called queer.

All the people were chattering in low voices; chairs
were moved noisily, and the slumbering juror opened
his weary eyes and troubled himself with an uncalled-
for effort to look as though he had been awake all the

time and did n't like the way things were going, at all. Horace got from the clerk the papers for which he had been waiting, and was passing out, when his Honor saw him and hailed him with an expressive grunt.

Gillespie, J., looked over his spectacles at Horace.

"Shall you see Judge Weeden at the office? Yes? Will you have the kindness to give him this — yes? If it 's no trouble to you, of course."

Gillespie, J., was not over-careful of the feelings of lawyers' clerks, as a rule; but he had that decent disinclination to act *ultra præscriptum* which marks the attitude of the well-bred man toward his inferiors in office. He knew that he had no business to use Weeden, Snowden & Gilfeather's clerk as a messenger in his private correspondence.

Horace understood him, took the letter, and allowed himself a quiet smile when he reached the crowded corridor.

What mattered, he thought, as his brisk feet clattered down the wide stairs of the rotunda, the petty insolence of office *now?* He was Gillespie's messenger to-day; but had not his young powers already received recognition from a greater than Gillespie? If Judge Gillespie lived long enough he should put his gouty old legs under Judge Walpole's mahogany, and prose over his port — yes, he should have port, like the relic of mellow old days that he was — of the times "when your father-in-law and I, Walpole, were boys together."

Ah, there you have the spell of the Red Silk Handkerchief!

It was a wonderful tale to Horace; for he saw it in

that wonderful light which shall shine on no man of us more than once in his life — on some of us not at all, Heaven help us ! — but, in the telling, it is a simple tale :

"The Golden-Mouthed Orator of St. Lawrence" was at the height of his fame in that period of storm and stress which had the civil war for its climax. His misfortune was to be drawn into a contest for which he was not equipped, and in which he had little interest. His sphere of action was far from the battle-ground of the day. The intense localism that bounded his knowledge and his sympathies had but one break — he had tasted in his youth the extravagant hospitality of the South, and he held it in grateful remembrance. So it happened that he was a trimmer, — a moderationist he called himself, — a man who dealt in optimistic generalities, and who thought that if everybody — the slaves included — would only act temperately and reasonably, and view the matter from the standpoint of pure policy, the differences of South and North could be settled as easily as, through his own wise intervention, the old turnip-field feud of Farmer Oliver and Farmer Bunker had been wiped out of existence.

His admirers agreed with him, and they sent him to Congress to fill the unexpired short term of their representative, who had just died in Washington of what we now know as a malarial fever. It was not to be expected, perhaps, that the Honorable Mr. Walpole would succeed in putting a new face on the great political question in the course of his first term ; but · they all felt sure that his first speech would startle men who had never heard better than what Daniel Webster had had to offer them.

But the gods were against the Honorable Mr. Walpole. On the day set for his great effort there was what the theatrical people call a counter-attraction. Majah Pike had come up from Mizourah, sah, to cane that demn'd Yankee hound, Chahles Sumnah, sah, — yes, sah, to thrash him like a dawg, begad! And all Washington had turned out to see the performance, which was set down for a certain hour, in front of Mr. Sumner's door.

There was just a quorum when the golden-mouthed member began his great speech, — an inattentive, chattering crowd, that paid no attention to his rolling rhetoric and rococo grandiloquence. He told the empty seats what a great country this was, and how beautiful was a middle policy, and he illustrated this with a quotation from Homer, in the original Greek (a neat novelty: Latin was fashionable for parliamentary use in Webster's time), with, for the benefit of the uneducated, the well-known translation by the great Alexander Pope, commencing:

> " To calm their passions with the words of Age,
> Slow from his seat arose the Pylian sage,
> Experienced Nestor, in Persuasion skilled,
> Words sweet as honey from his lips distilled " —

When Nestor and Mr. Walpole closed, there was no quorum. The member from New Jersey, who had engaged him in debate, was sleeping the sleep of honorable intoxication in his seat. Outside, all Washington was laughing and cursing. Majah Pike had not appeared.

It was the end of the golden-mouthed orator. His voice was never heard again in the House. His one speech was noticed only to be laughed at, and the news went home to his constituents. They showed that magnanimity which the poets tell us is an attribute of the bucolic character. They, so to speak, turned over the pieces of their broken idol with their cow-hide boots, and remarked that they had known it was clay, all along, and dern poor clay at that.

So the golden-mouthed went home, to try to make a ruined practice repair his ruined fortune; to give mortgages on his home to pay the debts his hospitality had incurred; to discuss with a few feeble old friends ways and means by which the war might have been averted; to beget a son of his old age, and to see the boy grow up in a new generation, with new ideas, new hopes, new ambitions, and a lifetime before him to make memories in.

They had little enough in common, but they came to be great friends as the boy grew older, for Horace inherited all his traits from the old man, except a certain stern energy which came from his silent, strong-hearted mother, and which his father saw with a sad joy.

Mr. Walpole sent his son to New York to study law in the office of Messrs. Weeden, Snowden & Gilfeather, who were a pushing young firm in 1850. Horace found it a very quiet and conservative old concern. Snowden and Gilfeather were dead; Weeden had been on the bench and had gone off the bench at the call of a "lucrative practice;" there were two new partners, whose names appeared only on the glass of the office door and in a corner of the letter-heads.

Horace read his law to some purpose. He became the managing clerk of Messrs. Weeden, Snowden & Gilfeather. This particular managing clerkship was one of unusual dignity and prospective profit. It meant, as it always does, great responsibility, little honor, and less pay. But the firm was so peculiarly constituted that the place was a fine stepping-stone for a bright and ambitious boy. One of the new partners was a business man, who had put his money into the concern in 1860, and who knew and cared nothing about law. He kept the books and managed the money, and was beyond that only a name on the door and a terror to the office-boys. The other new partner was a young man who made a specialty of collecting debts. He could wring gold out of the stoniest and barrenest debtor; and there his usefulness ended. The general practice of the firm rested on the shoulders of Judge Weeden, who was old, lazy, and luxury-loving, and who, to tell the honest truth, shirked his duties. Such a state of affairs would have wrecked a younger house; but Weeden, Snowden & Gilfeather had a great name, and the consequences of his negligent feebleness had not yet descended upon Judge Weeden's head.

That they would, in a few years, that the Judge knew it, and that he was quite ready to lean on a strong young arm, Horace saw clearly.

That his own arm was growing in strength he also saw; and the Judge knew that, too. He was Judge

Weeden's pet. All in the office recognized the fact. All, after reflection, concluded that it was a good thing that he was. New blood had to come into the firm sooner or later, and although it was not possible to watch the successful rise of this boy without a little natural envy and heart-burning, yet it was to be considered that Horace was one who would be honorable, just, and generous wherever fortune put him.

Horace was a gentleman. They all knew it. Barnes and Haskins, the business man and the champion collector, knew it down in the shallows of their vulgar little souls. Judge Weeden, who had some of that mysterious ichor of gentlehood in his wine-fed veins, knew it and rejoiced in it. And Horace — I can say for Horace that he never forgot it.

He was such a young prince of managing clerks that no one was surprised when he was sent down to Sand Hills, Long Island, to make preparations for the reorganization of the Great Breeze Hotel Company, and the transfer of the property known as the Breeze Hotel and Park to its new owners. The Breeze Hotel was a huge "Queen Anne" vagary which had, after the fashion of hotels, bankrupted its first owners, and was now going into the hands of new people, who were likely to make their fortunes out of it. The property had been in litigation for a year or so; the mechanics' liens were numerous, and the mechanics clamorous; and although the business was not particularly complicated, it needed careful and patient adjustment. Horace knew the case in every detail. He had drudged over it all the winter, with no especial hope of personal advantage, but simply because that was his way of working. He went down in June to the mighty barracks, and lived for a week in what would have been an atmosphere of paint and carpet-dye had it not been for the broad sea wind that blew through the five hundred open windows, and swept rooms and corridors with salty freshness. The summering folk had not arrived yet; there were only the new manager and his six score of raw recruits of clerks and servants. But Horace felt the warm blood coming back to his cheeks, that the town had somewhat paled, and he was quite content; and every day he went down to the long, lonely beach, and had a solitary swim, although the sharp water whipped his white skin to a biting red. The sea takes a long while to warm up to the summer, and is sullen about it.

He was to have returned to New York at the end of the week, and Haskins was to have taken his place; but it soon became evident to Weeden, Snowden & Gilfeather that the young man would attend to all that was to be done at Sand Hills quite as well as Mr. Haskins, or — quite as well as Judge Weeden himself, for that matter. He had to shoulder no great responsibility; the work was mostly of a purely clerical nature, vexatious enough, but simple. It had to be done on the spot, however; the original Breeze Hotel and Park Company was composed of Sand Hillers, and the builders were Sand Hillers, too, the better part of them. And there were titles to be searched; for the whole scheme was an ambitious splurge of Sand Hills pride and it had been undertaken and carried out in a reck-

less and foolish way. Horace knew all the wretched
little details of the case, and so Horace was entrusted
with duties such as do not often devolve upon a man
of his years; and he took up his burden proudly, and
with a glowing consciousness of his own strength.

Judge Weeden missed his active and intelligent
obedience in the daily routine of office business; but
the Judge thought it was just as well that Horace
should not know that fact. The young man's time
would come soon enough, and he would be none the
worse for serving his apprenticeship in modesty and
humility. The work entrusted to him was an honor
in itself. And then, there was no reason why poor
Walpole's boy should n't have a sort of half-holiday out
in the country, and enjoy his youth.

He was not recalled. The week stretched out. He
worked hard, found time to play, hugged his quickened
ambitions to his breast, wrote hopeful letters to the
mother at Montevista, made a luxury of his loneliness,
and felt a bashful resentment when the "guests"
of the hotel began to pour in from the outside
world.

For a day or two he fought shy of them. But these
first comers were lonely too, and not so much in love
with loneliness as he thought he was, and very soon he
became one of them. He had found out all the walks
and drives; he knew the times of the tides; he had
made friends with the fishermen for a league up and
down the coast, and he had amassed a store of valuable
hints as to where the first blue-fish might be expected
to run. Altogether he was a very desirable companion.

Besides, that bright, fresh face of his, and a certain look in it, made you friends with him at once, especially if you happened to be a little older, and to remember a look of the sort, lost, lost forever, in a boy's looking-glass.

So he was sought out, and he let himself be found, and the gregarious instinct in him waxed delightfully.

And then It came. Perhaps I should say She came; but it is not the woman we love; it is our dream of her. Sweet and tender, fair and good, she may be; but let it be honor enough for her that she has that glory about her face which our love kindles to the halo that lights many a man's life to the grave, though the face beneath it be dead or false.

I will not admit that it was only a pretty girl from Philadelphia who came to Sand Hills that first week in July. It was the rosy goddess herself, dove-drawn across the sea, in the warm path of the morning sun — although the tremulous, old-fashioned handwriting on the hotel register only showed that the early train had brought —

    " *Samuel Rittenhouse,*   *Philadelphia.*
    " *Miss Rittenhouse,*   *do.*"

It was the Honorable Samuel Rittenhouse, ex-Chief-Justice of Pennsylvania, the honored head of the Pennsylvania bar, and the legal representative of the Philadelphia contingent of the new Breeze Hotel and Park Company.

In the evening Horace called upon him in his rooms with a cumbersome stack of papers, and patiently

waded through explanations and repetitions until Mr.
Rittenhouse's testy courtesy — he had the nervous
manner of age apprehensive of youthful irreverence —
melted into a complacent and fatherly geniality.
Then, when the long task was done and his young
guest arose, he picked up the card that lay on the
table and trained his glasses on it.

"'H. K. Walpole?'" he said: "are you a New
Yorker, sir?"

"From the north of the State," Horace told him.

"Indeed, indeed. Why, let me see — you must be
the son of my old friend Walpole — of Otsego —
wasn't it?" said the old gentleman, still tentatively.

"St. Lawrence, sir."

"Yes, St. Lawrence — of course, of course. Why,
I knew your father well, years ago, sir. We were at
college together."

"At Columbia?"

"Yes — yes. Why, bless me," Judge Rittenhouse
went on, getting up to look at Horace: "you're the
image of your poor father at your age. A very brilliant
man, sir, a very able man. I did not see much of him
after we left college — I was a Pennsylvanian, and he
was from this State — but I have always remembered
your father with respect and regard, sir, — a very
able man. I think I heard of his death some years
ago."

"Three years ago," said Horace. His voice fell somewhat. How little to this old man of success was the
poor, unnoticed death of failure!

"Three years only!" repeated the judge, half apologetically; "ah, people slip away from each other in this world — slip away. But I'm glad to have met you, sir — very much pleased indeed. Rosamond!"

For an hour the subdued creaking of a rocking-chair by the window had been playing a monotonously pleasant melody in Horace's ears. Now and then a coy wisp of bright hair, or the reflected ghost of it, had flashed into view in the extreme lower left-hand corner of a mirror opposite him. Once he had seen a bit of white brow under it, and from time to time the low flutter of turning magazine leaves had put in a brief second to the rocking-chair.

All this time Horace's brains had been among the papers on the table; but something else within him had been swaying to and fro with the rocking-chair, and giving a leap when the wisp of hair bobbed into sight.

Now the rocking-chair accompaniment ceased, and the curtained corner by the window yielded up its treasure, and Miss Rittenhouse came forward, with one hand brushing the wisp of hair back into place, as if she were on easy and familiar terms with it. Horace envied it.

"Rosamond," said the judge: "This is Mr. Walpole, the son of my old friend Walpole. You have heard me speak of Mr. Walpole's father."

"Yes, papa," said the young lady, all but the corners of her mouth. And, oddly enough, Horace did not think of being saddened because this young woman had never heard of his father. Life was going on a new key, all of a sudden, with a hint of a melody to be unfolded that ran in very different cadences from the poor old tune of memory.

My heroine, over whose head some twenty summers had passed, was now in the luxuriant prime of her youthful beauty. Over a brow whiter than the driven snow fell clustering ringlets, whose hue —

That is the way the good old novelists and story-tellers of the Neville and Beverley days would have set out to describe Miss Rittenhouse, had they known her. Fools and blind! As if anyone could describe — as if a poet, even, could more than hint at what a man sees in a woman's face when, seeing, he loves.

For a few moments the talkers were constrained, and the talk was meagre and desultory. Then the Judge, who had been rummaging around among the dust-heaps of his memory, suddenly recalled the fact that he had once, in stage-coach days, passed a night at Montevista, and had been most hospitably treated. He dragged this fact forth, professed a lively remembrance of Mrs. Walpole, — "a fine woman, sir, your mother; a woman of many charms," — asked after her present health; and then, satisfied that he had acquitted himself of his whole duty, withdrew into the distant depths of his own soul and fumbled over the papers Horace had brought him, trying to familiarize himself with them, as a commander might try to learn the faces of his soldiers.

Then the two young people proceeded to find the key together, and began a most harmonious duet. Sand Hills was the theme. Thus it was that they had to go out on the balcony, where Miss Rittenhouse might gaze into the brooding darkness over the sea, and watch it wink a slow yellow eye with a humorous alternation of sudden and brief red. Thus, also, Horace had to explain how the lighthouse was constructed. This moved Miss Rittenhouse to scientific research. She must see how it was done. Mr. Walpole would be delighted to show her. Papa was so much interested in those mechanical matters. Mr. Walpole had a team and light wagon at his disposal, and would very much like to drive Miss Rittenhouse and her father over to the lighthouse. Miss Rittenhouse communicated this kind offer to her father. Her father saw what was expected of him, and dutifully acquiesced, like an obedient American father. Miss Rittenhouse had managed the Rittenhouse household and the head of the house of Rittenhouse ever since her mother's death.

Mr. Walpole really had a team at his disposal. He came from a country where people do not chase foxes, nor substitutes for foxes; but where they know and revere a good trotter. He had speeded many a friend's horse in training for the county fair. When he came to Sand Hills his soundness in the equine branch of a gentleman's education had attracted the attention of a horsey Sand-Hiller, who owned a showy team with a record of 2.37. This team was not to be trusted to the ordinary summer boarder on any terms; but the Sand-Hiller was thrifty and appreciative, and he lured Horace into hiring the turnout at a trifling rate, and thus captured every cent the boy had to spare, and got his horses judiciously exercised.

There was a showy light wagon to match the team, and the next day the light wagon, with Horace and the Rittenhouses in it, passed every carriage on the road to the lighthouse, where Miss Rittenhouse satisfied her scientific spirit with one glance at the lantern, after giving which glance she went outside and sat in the shade of the white tower with Horace, while the keeper showed the machinery to the Judge. Perhaps she went to the Judge afterward, and got him to explain it all to her.

Thus it began, and for two golden weeks thus it went on. The reorganized Breeze Hotel and Park Company met in business session on its own property, and Horace acted as a sort of honorary clerk to Judge Rittenhouse. The company, as a company, talked over work for a couple of hours each day. As a congregation of individuals, it ate and drank and smoked and played billiards and fished and slept the rest of the two dozen. Horace had his time pretty much to himself, or rather to Miss Rittenhouse, who monopolized it. He drove her to the village to match embroidery stuffs. He danced with her in the evenings when two stolidly soulful Germans, one with a fiddle and the other with a piano, made the vast dining-room ring and hum with Suppé and Waldteufel, — and this was to the great and permanent improvement of his waltzing. She taught him how to play lawn-tennis — he was an old-fashioned boy from the backwoods, and he thought that croquet was still in existence, so she had to teach him to play lawn-tennis — until he learned to play much better than she could. On the other hand, he was a fresh-water swimmer of rare wind and wiriness, and a young sea-god in the salt, as soon as he got used to its pungent strength. So he taught her to strike out beyond the surf-line, with broad, breath-long sweeps, and there to float and dive and make friends with the ocean. Even he taught her to fold her white arms behind her back, and swim with her feet. As he glanced over his shoulder to watch her following him, and to note the timorous, admiring crowd on the shore, she seemed a sea-bred Venus of Milo in blue serge.

I have known men to be bored by such matters. They made Horace happy. He was happiest, perhaps, when he found out that she was studying Latin. All the girls in Philadelphia were studying Latin that summer. They had had a little school Latin, of course; but now their aims were loftier. Miss Rittenhouse had brought with her a Harkness's Virgil, an Anthon's dictionary, an old Bullion & Morris, and — yes, when Horace asked her, she had brought an Interlinear; but she did n't mean to use it. They rowed out to the buoy, and put the Interlinear in the sea. They sat on the sands after the daily swim, and enthusiastically labored, with many an unclassic excursus, over P. V. Maronis Opera. Horace borrowed some books of a small boy in the hotel, and got up at five o'clock in the morning to run a couple of hundred lines or so ahead of his pupil, "getting out" a stint that would have made him lead a revolt had any teacher imposed it upon his class a few years before — for he was fresh enough from schooling to have a little left of the little Latin that colleges give.

He wondered how it was that he had never seen the poetry of the lines before. *Forsan et hæc olim meminisse juvabit* — for perchance it will joy us hereafter to remember these things! He saw the wet and weary sailors on the shore, hungrily eating, breathing hard after their exertions; he heard the deep cheerfulness of their leader's voice. The wind blew toward him over the pine barrens, as fresh as ever it blew past Dido's towers. A whiff of briny joviality and adventurous recklessness seemed to come from the page on his knee. And to him, also, had not She appeared who saw, hard by the sea, that pious old buccaneer-Lothario, so much tossed about on land and upon the deep?

This is what the moderns call a flirtation, and I do not doubt that it was called a flirtation by the moderns around these two young people. Somehow, though, they never got themselves "talked about," not even by the stranded nomads on the hotel verandas. Perhaps this was because there was such a joyous freshness and purity about both of them that it touched the hearts of even the slander-steeped old dragons who rocked all day in the shade, and embroidered tidies and talked ill of their neighbors. Perhaps it was because they also had that about them which the mean and vulgar mind always sneers at, jeers at, affects to disbelieve in, always recognizes and fears, — the courage and power of the finer strain. Envy in spit-curls and jealousy in a false front held their tongues, may be, because, though they knew that they, and even their male representatives, were safe from any violent retort, yet they recognized the superior force, and shrunk from it as the cur edges away from the quiescent whip.

There is a great difference, too, between the flirtations of the grandfatherless and the flirtations of the grandfathered. I wish you to understand that Mr. Walpole and Miss Rittenhouse did not *sprawl* through their flirtation, nor fall into that slipshod familiarity which takes all the delicate beauty of dignity and mutual respect out of such a friendship. Horace did not bow to the horizontal, and Miss Rittenhouse did not make a cheese-cake with her skirts when he held open the door for her to pass through; but the bond of courtesy between them was no less sweetly gracious on her side, no less finely reverential on his, than the taste of their grandparents' day would have exacted, — no less earnest, I think, that it was a little easier than puff and periwig might have made it.

Yet I also think, whatever was the reason that made the dragons let them alone, that a simple mother of the plain, old-fashioned style is better for a girl of Miss Rosamond Rittenhouse's age than any such precarious immunity from annoyance.

Ah, the holiday was short! The summons soon came for Horace. They went to the old church together for the second and last time, and he stood beside her, and they held the hymn-book between them.

Horace could not rid himself of the idea that they had stood thus through every Sunday of a glorious summer. The week before he had sung with her. He had a boyish baritone in him, one of those which may be somewhat extravagantly characterized as consisting wholly of middle register. It was a good voice for the campus, and, combined with that startling clearness of utterance which young collegians acquire, had been very effective in the little church. But to-day he had no heart to sing "Byefield" and "Pleyel"; he would rather stand beside her and feel his heart vibrate to the deep lower notes of her tender contralto, and his soul rise with the higher tones that soared upward from her pure young breast. And all the while he was making that act of devotion which — "uttered or unexpressed" — is, indeed, all the worship earth has ever known.

Once she looked up at him as if she asked, "Why don't you sing?" But her eyes fell quickly, he thought with a shade of displeasure in them at something they had seen in his. Yet as he watched her bent head, the cheek near him warmed with a slow, soft blush. He may only have fancied that her clear voice quivered a little with a tremolo not written in the notes at the top of the page.

And now the last day came. When the work-a-day world thrust its rough shoulder into Arcadia, and the hours of the idyll were numbered, they set to talking of it as though the two weeks that they had known each other were some sort of epitomized summer. Of course they were to meet again, in New York or in Philadelphia; and of course there were many days of summer in store for Miss Rittenhouse at Sand Hills, at Newport, and at Mount Desert; but Horace's brief season was closed, and somehow she seemed to fall readily into his way of looking upon it as a golden period of special and important value, their joint and exclusive property — something set apart from all the rest of her holiday, where there would be other men and other good times and no Horace.

It was done with much banter and merriment; but through it all Horace listened for delicate undertones that should echo to his ear the earnestness which sometimes rang irrepressibly in his own speech. In that marvellous instrument, a woman's voice, there are strange and fine possibilities of sound that may be the messengers of the subtlest intelligence or the sweet falterings of imperfect control. So Horace, with love to construe for him, did not suffer too cruelly from disappointment.

On the afternoon of that last day they sat upon the beach and saw the smoke of Dido's funeral pile go up, and they closed the dog's-eared Virgil, and, looking seaward, watched the black cloud from a coaling steamer mar the blinding blue where sea and sky blent at the horizon; watched it grow dull and faint, and fade away, and the illumined turquoise reassert itself.

Then he was for a farewell walk, and she, with that bright acquiescence with which a young girl can make companionship almost perfect, if she will, accepted it as an inspiration, and they set out. They visited together the fishermen's houses, where Horace bade good-bye to mighty-fisted friends, who stuck their thumbs inside their waistbands and hitched their trousers half way up to their blue-shirted arms, and said to him, "You come up here in Orgust, Mr. Walpole — say 'bout the fus' t' the third week 'n Orgust, 'n' we'll give yer some bloo-fishin' 't y' won't need t' lie about, neither." They all liked him, and heartily.

Old Rufe, the gruff hermit of the fishers, who lived a half-mile beyond the settlement, flicked his shuttle through the net he was mending, and did not look up as Horace spoke to him.

"Goin'?" he said; "waal, we 've all gotter go some time oruther. The' aint no real perma-nen-cy on this uth. Goin'? Waal, I'm "— he paused, and weighed the shuttle in his hand as though to aid him in balancing some important mental process. "Sho! I'm derned 'f I ain't sorry. Squall comin' up, an' don't y' make no mistake," he hurried on, not to be further committed to unguarded expression; "better look sharp, or y' 'll git a wettin'."

A little puff of gray cloud, scurrying along in the south-east, had spread over half the sky, and now came a strong, eddying wind. A big raindrop made a dark spot on the sand before them; another fell on Miss Rittenhouse's cheek, and then, with a vicious, uncertain patter, the rain began to come down.

"We 'll have to run for Poinsett's," said Horace, and stretched out his hand. She took it, and they ran.

Poinsett's was just ahead — a white house on a lift of land, close back of the shore-line, with a long garden stretching down in front, and two or three poplar trees. The wind was turning up the pale under-sides of grass-blade and flower leaf, and whipping the shivering poplars silver white. Cap'n Poinsett, late of Glouces-ter, Massachusetts, was tacking down the path in his pea-jacket, with his brass telescope tucked under his arm. He was making for the little white summer-house that overhung the shore; but he stopped to admire the two young people dashing up the slope toward him, for the girl ran with a splendid free stride that kept her well abreast of Horace's athletic lope.

"Come in," he said, opening the gate, and smiling on the two young faces, flushed and wet; "come right in out o' the rain. Be'n runnin', ain't ye? Go right int' the house. Mother!" he called, "here's Mr. Walpole 'n' his young lady. You'll hev to ex-cuse me; I'm a-goin' down t' my observa*tory*. I carn't foller the sea no longer myself, but I can look at them that dooz. There's my old woman — go right in."

He waddled off, leaving both of them redder than their run accounted for, and Mrs. Poinsett met them at the door, her arms folded in her apron.

"Walk right in," she greeted them; "the cap'n he mus' always go down t' his observa*tory*, 's he calls it, 'n' gape through thet old telescope of hisn, fust thing the 's a squall — jus's if he thought he was skipper of all Long Island. But you come right int' the settin'-room 'n' make yourselves to home. Dear me suz! 'f I'd 'a' thought I'd 'a' had company I'd 'a' tidied things up. I'm jus' 's busy *as* busy, gettin' supper ready; but don't you mind *me* — jus' you make yourselves to home," and she drifted chattering away, and they heard her in the distant kitchen amiably nagging the hired girl.

It was an old-time, low-ceiled room, neat with New England neatness. The windows had many panes of green flint glass, through which they saw the darkening storm swirl over the ocean and ravage the flower-beds near by.

And when they had made an end of watching Cap'n Poinsett in his little summer-house, shifting his long glass to follow each scudding sail far out in the darkness; and when they had looked at the relics of Cap'n Poinsett's voyages to the Orient and the Arctic, and at the cigar-boxes plastered with little shells, and at the wax fruit, and at the family trousers and bonnets in the album, there was nothing left but that Miss Rittenhouse should sit down at the old piano, bought for Amanda Jane in the last year of the war, and bring forth rusty melody from the yellowed keys.

"What a lovely voice she has!" thought Horace as she sang. No doubt he was right. I would take his word against that of a professor of music, who would have told you that it was a nice voice for a girl, and that the young woman had more natural dramatic expression than technical training.

They fished out Amanda Jane's music-books, and went through "Juanita," and the "Evergreen Waltz," and "Beautiful Isle of the Sea;" and, finding a lot of war songs, severally and jointly announced their determination to invade Dixie Land, and to annihilate Rebel Hordes; and adjured each other to remember Sumter and Baltimore, and many other matters that could have made but slight impression on their young minds twenty odd years before. Mrs. Poinsett, in the kitchen, stopped nagging her aid, and thought of young John Tarbox Poinsett's name on a great sheet of paper in the Gloucester post-office, one morning at the end of April, 1862, when the news came up that Farragut had passed the forts.

The squall was going over, much as it had come, only no one paid attention to its movements now, for the sun was out, trying to straighten up the crushed grass and flowers, and to brighten the hurrying waves, and to soothe the rustling agitation of the poplars.

They must have one more song. Miss Rittenhouse chose "Jeannette and Jeannot," and when she looked back at him with a delicious coy mischief in her eyes, and sang, —

> "There is no one left to love me now,
> And you too may forget" —

Horace felt something flaming in his cheeks and choking in his breast, and it was hard for him to keep from snatching those hands from the keys and telling her she knew better.

But he was man enough not to. He controlled himself, and made himself very pleasant to Mrs. Poinsett about not staying to supper, and they set out for the hotel.

The air was cool and damp after the rain.

"You've been singing," said Horace, "and you will catch cold in this air, and lose your voice. You must tie this handkerchief around your throat."

She took his blue silk handkerchief and tied it around her throat, and wore it until just as they were turning away from the shore, when she took it off to return to him; and the last gust of wind that blew that afternoon whisked it out of her hand, and sent it whirling a hundred yards out to sea.

"Now, don't say a word," said Horace; "it isn't of the slightest consequence."

But he looked very gloomy over it. He had made up his mind that that silk handkerchief should be the silk handkerchief of all the world to him, from that time on.

It was one month later that Mr. H. K. Walpole received, in care of Messrs. Weeden, Snowden & Gilfeather, an envelope postmarked Newport, containing a red silk handkerchief. His initials were neatly — nay, beautifully, exquisitely — stitched in one corner. But there was absolutely nothing about the package to show who sent it, and Horace sorrowed over this. Not that he was in any doubt; but he felt that it meant to say that he must not acknowledge it; and, loyally, he did not.

And he soon got over that grief. The lost handkerchief, whose origin was base and common, like other handkerchiefs, and whose sanctity was purely accidental — what was it to *this* handkerchief, worked by her for him?

This became the outward and visible sign of the inward and spiritual grace that had changed the boy's whole life. Before this he had had purposes and ambitions. He had meant to take care of his mother, to do well in the world, and to restore, if he could, the honor and glory of the home his father had left him. Here were duty, selfishness, and an innocent vanity. But

now he had an end in life, so high that the very seeking of it was a religion. Every thought of self was
flooded out of him, and what he sought he sought in a
purer and nobler spirit than ever before.

Is it not strange? A couple of weeks at the sea-side,
a few evenings under the brooding darkness of hotel
verandas, the going to and fro of a girl with a sweet
face, and this ineradicable change is made in the mind
of a man who has forty or fifty years before him wherein to fight the world, to find his place, to become a fac-
tor for good or evil.

And here we have Horace, with his heart full of love
and his head full of dreams, mooning over a silk handkerchief, in open court.

Not that he often took such chances. The daws of
humor peck at the heart worn on the sleeve; and quite
rightly, for that is no place for a heart. But in the
privacy of his modest lodging-house room he took the
handkerchief out, and spread it before him, and looked
at it, and kissed it sometimes, I suppose, — it seems
ungentle to pry thus into the sacredness of a boy's
love, — and, certainly, kept it in sight, working, studying, or thinking.

With all this, the handkerchief became somewhat
rumpled, and at last Horace felt that it must be
brought back to the condition of neatness in which he
first knew it. So, on a Tuesday, he descended to the
kitchen of his lodging-house, and asked for a flat-iron.
His good landlady, at the head of an industrious, plump-
armed Irish brigade, all vigorously smoothing out towels,
stared at him in surprise.

"If there's anything you want ironed, Mr. Walpole, bring it down here, and I'll be *more'n* glad to iron it for you."

Horace grew red, and found his voice going entirely out of his control, as he tried to explain that it wasn't for that — it wasn't for ironing clothes — he was sure nobody could do it but himself.

"Do you want it hot or cold?" asked Mrs. Wilkins, puzzled.

"Cold!" said Horace desperately. And he got it cold, and had to heat it at his own fire to perform his labor of love.

That was of a piece with many things he did. Of a piece, for instance, with his looking in at the milliners' windows and trying to think which bonnet would best become her — and then taking himself severely to task for dreaming that she would wear a ready-made bonnet. Of a piece with his buying two seats for the theatre, and going alone and fancying her next him, and glancing furtively at the empty place at the points where he thought she would be amused, or pleased, or moved.

What a fool he was! Yes, my friend, and so are you and I. And remember that this boy's foolishness did not keep him tossing, stark awake, through ghastly nights; did not start him up in the morning with a hot throat and an unrested brain; did not send him down to his day's work with the haunting, clutching, lurking fear that springs forward at every stroke of the clock, at every opening of the door. Perhaps you and I have known folly worse than his.

Through all the winter — the red handkerchief

cheered the hideous first Monday in October, and the Christmas holidays, when business kept him from going home to Montevista — he heard little or nothing of her. His friends in the city, or rather his father's friends, were all ingrained New Yorkers, dating from the provincial period, who knew not Philadelphia; and it was only from an occasional newspaper paragraph that he learned that Judge Rittenhouse and his daughter were travelling through the South, for the Judge's health. Of course, he had a standing invitation to call on them whenever he should find himself in Philadelphia; but they never came nearer Philadelphia than Washington, and so he never found himself in Philadelphia. He was not so sorry for this as you might think a lover should be. He knew that, with a little patience, he might present himself to Judge Rittenhouse as something more than a lawyer's managing clerk.

For, meanwhile, good news had come from home, and things were going well with him. Mineral springs had been discovered at Aristotle — mineral springs may be discovered anywhere in north New York, if you only try; though it is sometimes difficult to fit them with the proper Indian legends. The name of the town had been changed to Avoca, and there was already an Avoca Improvement Company, building a big hotel, advertising right and left, and prophesying that the day of Saratoga and Sharon and Richfield was ended. So the barrens between Montevista and Aristotle, skirting the railroad, suddenly took on a value. Hitherto they had been unsalable, except for taxes. For the most part they were an adjunct of the estate of Montevista; and in February Horace went up to St. Lawrence County and began the series of sales that was to realize his father's most hopeless dream, and clear Montevista of all incumbrances.

How pat it all came, he thought, as, on his return trip, the train carried him past the little old station, with its glaring new sign, AVOCA, just beyond the broad stretch of " Squire Walpole's bad land," now sprouting with the surveyors' stakes. After all was paid off on the old home, there would be enough left to enable him to buy out Haskins, who had openly expressed his desire to get into a "live firm," and who was willing to part with his interest for a reasonable sum down, backed up by a succession of easy installments. And Judge Weeden had intimated, as clearly as dignity would permit, his anxiety that Horace should seize the opportunity.

Winter was still on the Jersey flats on the last day of March; but Horace, waiting at a little "flag station," found the air full of crude prophecies of spring. He had been searching titles all day, in a close and gloomy little town-hall, and he was glad to be out-of-doors again, and to think that he should be back in New York by dinner time, for it was past five o'clock.

But a talk with the station-master made the prospect less bright. No train would stop there until seven.

Was there no other way of getting home? The lonely guardian of the Gothic shanty thought it over, and found that there was a way. He talked of the trains as though they were whimsical creatures under his charge.

"The's a freight comin' down right now," he said, meditatively, "but I can't do nothin' with her. She's gotter get along mighty lively to keep ahead of the Express from Philadelphia till she gets to the junction and goes on a siding till the Express goes past. And as to the Express — why, I couldn't no more flag her than if she was a cyclone. But I tell you what you do. You walk right down to the junction — 'bout a mile 'n' a half down — and see if you can't do something with number ninety-seven on the other road. You see, she goes on to New York on our tracks, and she mostly's in the habit of waiting at the junction 'bout — say five to seven minutes, to give that Express from Philadelphia a fair start. That Express has it pretty much her own way on this road, for a fact. You go down to the junction — walk right down the line — and you'll get ninety-seven — there ain't no kind of doubt about it. You can't see the junction; but it's just half a mile beyont that curve down there."

So there was nothing to be done but to walk to the junction. The railroad ran a straight, steadily descending mile on the top of a high embankment, and then suddenly turned out of sight around a ragged elevation. Horace buttoned his light overcoat, and tramped down the cinder-path between the tracks.

Yes, spring was coming. The setting sun beamed a soft, hopeful red over the shoulder of the ragged elevation; light, drifting mists rose from the marsh land below him, and the last low rays struck a vapory opal through them. There was a warm, almost prismatic purple hanging over the outlines of the hills and woods far to the east. The damp air, even, had a certain languid warmth in it; and though there was snow in the little hollows at the foot of the embankment, and bits of thin whitish ice were in the swampy pools, it was clear enough to Horace that spring was at hand. Spring — and then summer; and, by the sea or in the mountains, the junior partner of the house of Weeden, Snowden & Gilfeather might hope to meet once more with Judge Rittenhouse's daughter.

The noise of the freight-train, far up the track behind him, disturbed Horace's springtime revery. A forethought of rocking gravel-cars scattering the overplus of their load by the way, and of reeking oil-tanks, filling the air with petroleum, sent him down the embankment to wait until the way was once more clear.

The freight-train went by and above him with a long-drawn roar and clatter, and with a sudden fierce crash, and the shriek of iron upon iron, at the end, and the last truck of the last car came down the embankment, tearing a gully behind it, and ploughed a grave for itself in the marsh ten yards ahead of him.

And, looking up, he saw a twisted rail raising its head like a shining serpent above the dim line of the embankment. A furious rush took Horace up the slope. A quarter of a mile below him the freight-train was slipping around the curve. The fallen end of the last car was beating and tearing the ties. He heard the shrill creak of the brakes and the frightened whistle of the locomotive. But the grade was steep, and it was hard to stop. And if they did stop they were half a mile from the junction — half a mile from their only chance of warning the Express.

Horace heard in his ears the station-master's words: "She's gotter get along mighty lively to keep ahead of the Express from Philadelphia."

"Mighty lively — mighty lively," — the words rang through his brain to the time of thundering car-wheels.

He knew where he stood. He had made three-quarters of the straight mile. He was three-quarters of a mile, then, from the little station. His overcoat was off in half a second. Many a time had he stripped, with that familiar movement, to trunks and sleeveless shirt, to run his mile or his half-mile; but never had such a thirteen hundred yards lain before him, up such a track, to be run for such an end.

The sweat was on his forehead before his right foot passed his left.

His young muscles strove and stretched. His feet struck the soft, unstable path of cinders with strong, regular blows. His tense forearms strained upward from his sides. Under his chest, thrown outward from his shoulders, was a constricting line of pain. His wet face burnt. There was a fire in his temples, and at every breath of his swelling nostrils something throbbed behind his eyes. The eyes saw nothing but a dancing dazzle of tracks and ties, through a burning blindness. And his feet beat, beat, beat till the shifting cinders seemed afire under him.

That is what this human machine was doing, going

at this extreme pressure; every muscle, every breath, every drop of blood alive with the pain of this intense stress. Looking at it you would have said, "A fleet, light-limbed young man, with a stride like a deer, throwing the yards under him in fine style." All we know about the running other folks are making in this world!

Half-way up the track Horace stopped short, panting hard, his heart beating like a crazy drum, a nervous shiver on him. Up the track there was a dull whirr, and he saw the engine of the express-train slipping down on him—past the station already.

The white mists from the marshes had risen up over the embankment. The last rays of the sunset shot through them, brilliant and blinding. Horace could see the engine; but would the engineer see him, waving his hands in futile gestures, in time to stop on that slippery, sharp grade? And of what use would be his choking voice when the dull whirr should turn into a roar? For a moment, in his hopeless disappointment, Horace felt like throwing himself in the path of the train, like a wasted thing that had no right to live, after so great a failure.

As will happen to those who are stunned by a great blow, his mind ran back mechanically to the things nearest his heart, and in a flash he went through the two weeks of his life. And then, before the thought had time to form itself, he had brought a red silk handkerchief from his breast, and was waving it with both hands, a fiery crimson in the opal mist.

Seen. The whistle shrieked; there was a groan and

a creak of brakes, the thunder of the train resolved itself into various rattling noises, the engine slipped slowly by him, and slowed down, and he stood by the platform of the last car as the express stopped.

There was a crowd around Horace in an instant. His head was whirling, but in a dull way he said what he had to say. An officious passenger, who would have explained it all to the conductor if the conductor had waited, took the deliverer in his arms — for the boy was near fainting — and enlightened the passengers who flocked around.

Horace hung in his embrace, too deadly weak even to accept the offer of one of the dozen flasks that were thrust at him. Nothing was very clear in his mind; as far as he could make out, his most distinct impression was of a broad, flat beach, a blue sea and a blue sky, a black steamer making a black trail of smoke across them, and a voice soft as an angel's reading Latin close by him. Then he opened his eyes and saw the woman of the voice standing in front of him.

"Oh, Richard," he heard her say, "it's Mr. Walpole!"

Horace struggled to his feet. She took his hand in both of hers and drew closer to him; the crowd falling back a little, seeing that they were friends.

"What can I ever say to thank you?" she said. "You have saved our lives. It's not so much for myself, but" — she blushed faintly, and Horace felt her hands tremble on his; "Richard — my husband — we were married to-day, you know — and" —

Something heavy and black came between Horace and life for a few minutes. When it passed away he straightened himself up out of the arms of the officious passenger and stared about him, mind and memory coming back to him. The people around looked at him oddly. A brakeman brought him his overcoat, and he stood unresistingly while it was slipped on him. Then he turned away and started down the embankment.

"Hold on!" cried the officious passenger excitedly; "we're getting up a testimonial"—

Horace never heard it. How he found his way he never cared to recall; but the gas was dim in the city streets, and the fire was out in his little lodging-house room when he came home; and his narrow white bed knows all that I cannot tell of his tears and his broken dreams.

"Walpole," said Judge Weeden, as he stood between the yawning doors of the office safe, one morning in June, "I observe that you have a private package here. Why do you not use the drawer of our — our late associate, Mr. Haskins? It is yours now, you know. I'll put your package in it." He poised the heavily · sealed envelope in his hand. "Very odd *feeling* package, Walpole. Remarkably soft!" he said. "Well, bless me, it's none of my business, of course. Horace, how much you look like your father!"

THE SEVEN CONVERSATIONS

OF

DEAR JONES AND BABY VAN RENSSELAER.

BY BRANDER MATTHEWS AND H. C. BUNNER.

I.

THE FIRST CONVERSATION.

TUESDAY, February 14, 1882.

THE band was invisible, but, unfortunately, not in-
audible. It was in the butler's pantry, playing
Waldteufel's latest waltz, " Süssen Veilchen." The
English butler, who resented the intrusion of the Ger-
man leader, was introducing an *obbligato* unforeseen by
the composer. This was the second of Mrs. Martin's
charming Tuesdays in February. Mrs. Martin herself,
fondly and familiarly known as the " Duchess of Washington Square," stopped a young man as he was making a desperate rush for his overcoat, then reposing
under three strata of late comers' outer garments in the
second-floor back, and said to him :

"O Dear Jones "— the Duchess always called him
Dear Jones — " I want to introduce you to Baby Van
Rensselaer — Phyllis Van Rensselaer, you know — they
always called her Baby Van Rensselaer, though I 'm
sure I don't know why — Phyllis is such a lovely name

—don't you think so?—and your grandfathers were such friends." [Dear Jones executed an *ex post facto* condemnation upon his ancestor and hers.] "You know Major Van Rensselaer was your grandfather's partner until that unfortunate affair of the embezzlement— O Baby dear—there you are, are you? I was wondering where you were all this time. This is Mr. Jones, dear, one of your grandfather's most intimate friends. Oh, I don't mean that, of course—you know what I mean—and I do so want you two to know each other."

Dear Jones: What in the name of the prophet does the Duchess mean by introducing me to More Girls?

Baby Van Rensselaer: I do wish the Duchess would n't insist on tiring me out with slim young men; I never can tell one from the other.

These remarks were not uttered. They remained in the privacy of the inner consciousness. What they really said was:

Dear Jones [*inarticulately*]: Miss Van Rensselaer.

Baby Van Rensselaer [*inattentively*]: Yes, it *is* rather warm. . . .

And they drifted apart in the crowd.

II.

THE SECOND CONVERSATION.

Thursday, April 13, 1882.

Of course, Dear Jones was the last to arrive of the favored children of the world who had been invited to dine at Judge Gillespie's "to meet the Lord Bishop

of Barset," just imported from England per steamer
" Servia." In the hall, the butler, whose appearance
was even more dignified and clerical than the Bishop's,
handed Dear Jones an unsealed communication.

DEAR JONES [*examining the contents*]: Who in
Heligoland is Miss Van Rensselaer?

As Dear Jones entered, Mrs. Sutton — the Judge's
daughter, you know — married Charley Sutton, who
came from San Francisco — Mrs. Sutton gave a little
sigh of relief, nodded to the butler, and said in per-
functory answer to the apologies Dear Jones had not
made: "Oh, no; you're not a bit late — we haven't
been waiting for you at all — the Bishop has only just
come "— (confidentially in his ear) "I've given you a
charming girl." [Dear Jones shuddered: he knew what
that generally meant.] "You know Baby Van Rensselaer? Of course — there she is — now, go — and do
be bright and clever." And after thus handicapping
an inoffensive young man, she took the Bishop's arm in
the middle of his ante-prandial anecdote.

DEAR JONES [*marching to his fate*]: It's the
Duchess's girl again, by Jove! It's lucky Uncle
Larry is going to take me off at ten sharp.

BABY VAN RENSSELAER: Why, it's *that* Mr.
Jones!

These remarks were not uttered. They remained in
the privacy of the inner consciousness. What they
really said was : ·

DEAR JONES [*with audacious hypocrisy*]: Of course,
you don't remember me, Miss Van Rensselaer. . . .

Baby Van Rensselaer [*trumping his card unabashed*]: I really don't quite. . . .

Dear Jones [*offering his arm*]: Er . . . don't you remember the Duch — Mrs. Martin's — that hideously rainy afternoon, just before Lent?

Here there was a gap in the conversation as the procession took up its line of march, and moved through a narrow passage into the dining-room.

Dear Jones [*making a brave dash at the "bright and clever"*]: Well, in *my* house, the door into the dining-room shall be eighteen feet wide.

Baby Van Rensselaer [*literal, stern, and cold*]: Are you building a house, Mr. Jones?

Dear Jones [*calmly*]: I am at present, Miss Van Rensselaer, building — let me see — four — five — seven houses.

Baby Van Rensselaer [*coldly and suspecting flippancy*]: Ah, indeed — are you a billionaire?

Dear Jones: No; I'm an architect.

Baby Van Rensselaer [*in confusion*]: Oh, I'm sure I beg your pardon —

Dear Jones: You need n't. I should n't be at all ashamed to be a billionaire.

Baby Van Rensselaer: Oh, of course not — I did n't mean *that* —

Dear Jones [*unguardedly*]: Well, if it comes to that; I'm not ashamed of my architecture either.

Baby Van Rensselaer [*calmly*]: Indeed? I have never seen any of it.

Dear Jones: You sit here, I think. This is your card with the little lady in the powdered wig — a cherubic Madame de Staël.

BABY VAN RENSSELAER: And this is yours with a Cupid in a basket — a nineteenth century Moses.

DEAR JONES [*taking his seat beside her*]: Talking about dinner cards — and billionaires, you heard of that dinner old Creasers gave to fifty-two of his friends of the new dispensation. I believe there *was* one poor fellow there whose wife had only half a peck of diamonds. He assembled his hordes in the picture-gallery, as the dining-room wasn't large enough — you see, I didn't build *his* house. And to carry out the novelty of the thing, his dinner cards were —

BABY VAN RENSSELAER: Playing-cards?

DEAR JONES: Just so — but they were painted, "hand-painted" on satin.

BABY VAN RENSSELAER: And what did he take for himself — the king of diamonds?

DEAR JONES: For the only time in his life he forgot himself — and he had to put up with the Joker.

BABY VAN RENSSELAER: What sort of people were there?

DEAR JONES: Very good sort, indeed. There was a M. Meissonnier and M. Gérôme and a M. Corot — besides the man who sold them to him.

Everybody knows how a conversation runs on at dinner, when it does run on. On this occasion it ran on for seventy minutes and six courses. Dear Jones and Baby Van Rensselaer discussed the usual topics and the usual bill-of-fare. Then, as the butler served the bombe *glacée à la Demidoff* —

BABY VAN RENSSELAER: Oh, I'm so glad you liked her. We were at school together, you know, and she was with us when we went up the Saguenay last August.

DEAR JONES: Why, *I* went up the Saguenay last August.

BABY VAN RENSSELAER [*earnestly*]: And we didn't meet? How miserably absurd!

DEAR JONES: I'll tell you whom I did meet — your father's partner, Mr. Hitchcock. He had his daughter with him, too — a very bright girl. You know her, of course.

BABY VAN RENSSELAER [*coldly*]: I have heard she is quite clever. [A pause.] The Hitchcocks — I believe — go more in the — New England set. I have met her brother, though — Mr. Mather Hitchcock. . .

DEAR JONES: Mat Hitchcock; that little cad?

BABY VAN RENSSELAER: Is he a little cad? I thought he was rather — bright.

After this, conversation was desultory; and soon the male guests were left to their untrammeled selves, tobacco and the Bishop. At eleven minutes past ten, in the vestibule of Judge Gillespie's house, a young man and a man not so young were buttoning their overcoats and lighting their cigarettes. In the parlor behind them a soft contralto voice was lingering on the rich, deep notes of "Der Asra," the sweetest song of Jewish inspiration, the song of Heine and of Rubinstein. They paused a moment as the voice died away in

"Und mein Stamm sind jene Asra,
Welche sterben wenn sie lieben!"

The man not so young said: "Well, come along. What are you waiting for?"

DEAR JONES: What the devil are you in such a hurry for, Uncle Larry? It looked abominably rude to leave those people in that way!"

III.

THE THIRD CONVERSATION.

TUESDAY, May 30, 1882.

As the first band of the Decoration Day procession struck up "Marching through Georgia" and marched past Uncle Larry's house, a cheerfully expectant party filed out of the parlor windows upon the broad stone balcony, draped with the flag that had floated over the building for the four long years the day commemorated. Uncle Larry had secured the Duchess to matronize the annual gathering of young friends, the final friendly meeting before the flight out of town; and many of those who accepted him as the universal uncle had accepted also this invitation. Dear Jones and Baby Van Rensselaer were seated in the corner of the balcony that caught the southern sun, Baby Van Rensselaer, in Uncle Larry's own study chair, while Dear Jones was comfortably and gracefully perched on the broad brown-stone railing of the balcony.

BABY VAN RENSSELAER: Now, *does n't* that music make your heart leap?

DEAR JONES: M'— yes.

BABY VAN RENSSELAER: You know I haven't the

least bit of sympathy with that affected talk about not being moved by these things, and thinking it vulgar and all that. I'm proud to say I love my country, and I do love to see my country's soldiers. Don't you?"

DEAR JONES: M'—yes.

BABY VAN RENSSELAER: Of course, I can't really remember anything about the war, but I try to pretend to myself that I do remember when I was held up at the window to see the troops marching back from the grand review at Washington. (*Rather more softly.*) Mama told me about it often before she died. And "Marching through Georgia" always makes the tears come to my eyes; don't it yours?

DEAR JONES: M'—yes.

BABY VAN RENSSELAER: "Yes!" How queerly you say that!

DEAR JONES (*grimly*): I'm rather more inclined to cry when the band makes

> "Stream and forest, hill and strand,
> Reverberate with 'Dixie.'"

BABY VAN RENSSELAER (*coldly*): I'm afraid, Mr. Jones, I do not understand you. And you appear to have a very peculiar feeling about these things.

DEAR JONES [*rather absently*]: Well, yes, it is rather a matter of feeling with me. Weak, I suppose — but the fact is, Miss Van Rensselaer, it just breaks me up to see all this. You know, the war hit me pretty hard. I lost my brother in hospital after Seven Pines — and then I lost my father, the best friend I ever had, at Gettysburg, on the hill, you know, when he was lead-

ing his regiment, and his men could n't make him stay
back. So, you see, I would n't have come here at all
to-day if — if —

BABY VAN RENSSELAER: Oh, Mr. Jones, I'm *so
sorry.*

DEAR JONES [*surprised*]: Sorry? Why?

BABY VAN RENSSELAER: I did n't quite understand you — but I do now. Why, you 're taking off
your hat. What is it? Oh, the battle-flags!

DEAR JONES: My father's regiment.

BABY VAN RENSSELAER [*to herself*]: I wonder
if that is the regiment I saw coming back from Washington?

IV.

THE FOURTH CONVERSATION.

TUESDAY, August 22, 1882.

The train rattled hotly along on its sultry journey
from one end of Long Island to the other, a journey the
half of which it had nearly accomplished with much
fuss and fret. Leaving his impediments of travel in
the smoker, Dear Jones entered the forward end of the
parlor car in search of an uncontaminated glass of
water. As he set down the glass he glanced along the
car, and his manner changed at once. He opened the
door for an instant and threw on the down track his
half-smoked cigarette; and then, smiling pleasantly, he
walked firmly down the car, past a rustic bridal couple,
and took a vacant seat just in front of Baby Van
Rensselaer.

BABY VAN RENSSELAER: Why, Mr. Jones!

DEAR JONES: Why, Miss Van Rensselaer!

BABY VAN RENSSELAER: Who would have thought of seeing you here in this hot weather?

DEAR JONES: Can I have this seat or is it that I *mank* at the *convenances* — as the French say?

BABY VAN RENSSELAER: It's Uncle Larry's chair — he's gone back to talk to one of his vestrymen — he's taking me to Shelter Island.

DEAR JONES: Shelter Island? How long are you going to stay there?

BABY VAN RENSSELAER: And where are you going?

DEAR JONES: I'm going to Sag Harbor to build a house for one of my billionaires.

BABY VAN RENSSELAER: Sag Harbor? What an extraordinary place for a house.

DEAR JONES: Oh, that's nothing. Last year I had to build a house up in Chemung county.

BABY VAN RENSSELAER: Chemung?

DEAR JONES [*spelling it*]: C-h-e-m-u-n-g' — accent on the mung. You probably call it Cheémung, but it is really Sh'mung.

BABY VAN RENSSELAER: Where is it? and how do you get there?

DEAR JONES: By the *Chemung de fer*, of course.

BABY VAN RENSSELAER: Oh, Mr. Jones.

DEAR JONES: You see, my mind is relaxed by the effort to build a house on the model of the one occupied by the old woman who lived in a shoe — and that variety of early English architecture is very wearing on the taste. What sort of a house is it you are going to at

Shelter Island? And how long are you going to stay there?

BABY VAN RENSSELAER: Oh, it's a stupid, old-fashioned place [*pause*]. Do you think that bride is pretty? I have been watching them ever since we left New York. They have been to town on their wedding-trip.

DEAR JONES: She is ratherish pretty. And he's a shrewd fellow and likely to get on. I should n't wonder if he was the chief wire-puller of his "deestrick."

BABY VAN RENSSELAER: A village Hampden?

DEAR JONES: Some day he'll withstand the little tyrant of the fields and lead a revolt against the garden-sass monopoly, and so sail into the legislature. I fear the bride is destined to ruin her digestion in an Albany boarding-house, while the groom gives his days and nights to affairs of state.

Here the train slackened its speed as it approached a small station from which shrill notes of music arose.

BABY VAN RENSSELAER: Look, the bride is going to leave us.

DEAR JONES: He lives here, and the local fife and drum corps have come to welcome him home. Dinna ye hear that strident "Hail to the Chief," they have just executed?

BABY VAN RENSSELAER: How proudly she looks up at him! I think the band ought to play something for her — but they are men, and they'll never think of it.

DEAR JONES: You cannot expect much tact from two fifes and a bass drum, but unless my ears deceive me they have greeted the bride with a well-meant attempt at "Home, Sweet Home."

BABY VAN RENSSELAER:

> " And each responsive soul has heard
>   That plaintive note's appealing.
> So deeply ' Home, Sweet Home' has stirred
>   The hidden founts of feeling."

DEAR JONES [*surprised*]: Why — how did you know that poem?

BABY VAN RENSSELAER: Oh, I heard somebody quote it last Decoration Day — I don't know who — it struck me as very pretty and I looked it up.

DEAR JONES [*pleased*]: Oh, I remember. It has always been a favorite of mine.

BABY VAN RENSSELAER [*coldly*]: Indeed?

DEAR JONES [*as the train starts again*]: Bride and groom, fife and drum, fade away from sight and hearing. I wonder if we shall ever think of them again?

BABY VAN RENSSELAER: I shall, I'm sure. She was so pretty. And, besides, the music was lively. I shan't have anything half as amusing as that at Shelter Island.

DEAR JONES: Don't you like it, then?

BABY VAN RENSSELAER: Oh, dear no! I shall be glad to get away to 'my aunt's place at Watch Hill. It's very poky indeed, at Shelter Island (*sighs*). And to think that I shall have to spend just two weeks of primness and propriety there.

DEAR JONES: Just two weeks? Ah!

V.

THE FIFTH CONVERSATION.

TUESDAY, September 5, 1882. (Afternoon.)

ALTHOUGH it is difficult to tell the length from the breadth of the small steamer that plies between Sag Harbor and New London, it is safe to assume that it was the bow that was pointing away from the Shelter Island dock as Baby Van Rensselaer stepped out of the cabin and Dear Jones walked up to her, lifting his hat with an expression of surprise on his face that might have been better, considering that he had rehearsed it a number of times since he left Sag Harbor.

BABY VAN RENSSELAER: Why, Mr. Jones!

DEAR JONES [*forgetting his lines, and improvising*]: How—how—odd we should meet again just here. Funny, isn't it?

BABY VAN RENSSELAER: It is exceedingly humorous.

DEAR JONES: I did not tell you, did I!—when I saw you on the train, you know—that I had to go to New London, after I'd finished my work at Sag Harbor.

BABY VAN RENSSELAER [*uncompromisingly*]: I don't think you said anything about New London at all.

DEAR JONES: I probably said the Pequot House. It's the same thing, you know. I have to go to New London to inspect the Race Rock lighthouse—you've heard of the famous lighthouse at Race Rock, of course.

BABY VAN RENSSELAER: I don't think its fame has reached me.

DEAR JONES: It's a very curious structure, indeed. And, the fact is, one of my — my billionaires — wants a lighthouse. He has an extraordinary notion of building a lighthouse near his place on the seashore — a lighthouse of his own. Odd idea, isn't it?

BABY VAN RENSSELAER: It is a very odd proceeding altogether, I should say.

DEAR JONES: I suppose you mean that *I* am a very odd proceeding. Well, I will confess, and throw myself on your mercy. I *did* hope to meet you — and the Duch — Mrs. Martin. After two weeks of the society of billionaires, I think I'm excusable. . . . [*A painful pause.*] And I *had* to go to Race Rock, so I got off a day earlier than I had meant to, by cutting one of the turrets out of my original plan — he didn't mind — there are eleven left — and — and — will you forgive me?

BABY VAN RENSSELAER: Really, I have nothing to forgive, Mr. Jones. I've no doubt my aunt will be very glad to see you.

DEAR JONES: Ah — how *is* Mrs. Martin?

BABY VAN RENSSELAER. She is in the cabin. She is quite well at present; but she is always very nervous about sea-sickness, and she prefers to lie down. I must go in and sit with her.

DEAR JONES [*quickly*]: Indeed — I didn't know Mrs. Martin suffered from sea-sickness. She's crossed the ocean so many times, you know. How many is it?

BABY VAN RENSSELAER: Six, I think.

DEAR JONES: No; eight, is n't it? I'm almost sure it's eight.

BABY VAN RENSSELAER: Very possibly. But she is a great sufferer. I must go and see how she is.

DEAR JONES: Yes, we'll go. I want to see Mrs. Martin. One of the disadvantages of the summer season is that one can't see the Duchess at regular intervals to exchange gossip.

BABY VAN RENSSELLAER: Well, if you have any confidential gossip for the Duchess, I will wait here until you come out. I want to get all the fresh air possible, if I have to sit in the cabin for the rest of the trip.

DEAR JONES [*asserting himself*]: Very well. I have the contents of four letters from Newport to pour into the Duchess's ear. You know I was staying at the Hitchcocks' for a fortnight, before I went to Sag Harbor.

He went into the stuffy little cabin, where the Duchess was lying on a bench, in a wilderness of shawls. Baby Van Rensselaer waited a good half-hour, but heard no sound of returning footsteps from that gloomy cave. Finally she went in to investigate, and was told by the Duchess that "Dear Jones has gone after, or whatever you call it, to smoke a cigar." Baby Van Rensselaer made up her mind that under those circumstances she would go forward and read her book. She also made up her mind that Mr. Jones was extremely rude. His rudeness, she found, as she sat reading at the bow of the boat, really spoiled her book. She knew that she ought not to let such little things annoy her; but then, it was a very stupid chapter, and the fresh sea breeze blew the pages back and forward, and her veil would not stay over her hair, and she always had hated traveling, and it was so disagreeable to have people behave in that way — especially people — well, any people. Just here she turned her head, and saw Dear Jones advancing from the cabin with a bright and smiling face.

Baby Van Rensselaer [*about to rise*]: My aunt wants me, I suppose.

Dear Jones: Not at all — not in the least — at present. I just came through the cabin — on tiptoe — and she was fast asleep. In fact, not to speak it profanely, she was — she was audible.

Baby Van Rensselaer: Oh!

Dear Jones: I'm glad to see you're getting the benefit of the fresh air.

Baby Van Rensselaer: I was afraid of waking my aunt with the rustling of the leaves of my book, so I came out here.

Dear Jones: I'm glad you did. It would be a shame for you to have to sit in that close cabin. That's the reason I didn't come back to you when I left Mrs. Martin. I played a pious fraud on you for the benefit of your health.

Baby Van Rensselaer: You were very considerate.

Dear Jones [*enthusiastically*]: Oh, not at all.

Baby Van Rensselaer [*calmly*]: And if you'll

excuse me, I'll finish my book. I can't read in the cabin.

Baby Van Rensselaer resumed her reading and found the book improved a little. After a while she looked up and saw Dear Jones sitting on the rail, meekly twirling his thumbs.

BABY VAN RENSSELAER [*after an effort at silence*]: Don't be so ridiculously absurd. What are you doing there?

DEAR JONES: I'm waiting to be spoken to.

Baby Van Rensselaer smiled. The boat had just swung out of the jaws of the bay. Overhead was the full glory of a sky which made one believe that there never was such a thing as a cloud. And they sped along over the sea of water in a sea of light. Just then there came from the depths under the cabin the rise and fall of a measured, mocking melody, high and clear as the notes of a lark.

BABY VAN RENSSELAER: Why, that must be a bird whistling — only birds don't whistle "Amaryllis."

DEAR JONES: 'Tisn't a bird — it's an engineer.

BABY VAN RENSSELAER: An engineer?

DEAR JONES: A grimy engineer. Quite a pathetic story, too. Some of the Sag Harbor people took him up as a boy. He had a wonderful ear and an extraordinary tenor voice. They were going to make a Mario of him. They paid for his education in New York, and then sent him over to Paris to the Conservatory to be finished off. And he hadn't been there six weeks before he caught the regular Paris pleurisy

—it's an *article de Paris,* you know, and lost his voice utterly and hopelessly.

BABY VAN RENSSELAER: Oh!

DEAR JONES: And so he had to come back and engineer for his living.

BABY VAN RENSSELAER: How very sad. Now I can scarcely bear to hear him whistle.

DEAR JONES [*to himself*]: Well, I did n't mean to produce that effect. [*To her.*] Oh, he does n't mind it a bit. Hear him now.

The engineer was executing a series of brilliant variations on the "Air du Roi Louis XIII.," melting by ingenious gradations into the "Babies on our Block."

DEAR JONES [*hastily*]: Race Rock lies over that way. You can't see it yet — but you will after a while.

BABY VAN RENSSELAER: Oh, then there *is* a Race Rock?

DEAR JONES: Why, certainly. . . .

With this starter, it may readily be understood that a man of Dear Jones's fecundity of intellect and fine imaginative powers was able to fill the greater part of the afternoon with fluent conversation. Two or three times Baby Van Rensselaer made futile attempts to go into the cabin to see how the Duchess was sleeping; but as many times she forgot her errand. There was a fair breeze blowing from the northeast, but the sea was smooth, and the little boat scarcely rocked on the long, low waves. It was getting toward four o'clock when there was a sudden stoppage of the engineer's whistling, and of the machinery of the boat. Baby Van Rensselaer sent Dear Jones back to inquire into the cause, for they were alone on the broad sea, with only a tantalizing glimpse of New London harbor stretching out welcoming arms of green, with the Groton monument stuck like a huge clothes-pin on the left arm. Dear Jones came back, trying hard to look decently perturbed and gloomy, but with a barbarian joy lighting up his bronzed features.

BABY VAN RENSSELAER: What is it?

DEAR JONES: The machinery is on a dead centre. And the whistling engineer says that he'll have to wait until he can get into port and hitch a horse to the crank to start her off again.

BABY VAN RENSSELAER: But how are we to get into port?

DEAR JONES: The whistling engineer further says that we are now drifting toward Watch Hill.

BABY VAN RENSSELAER: That's just where we want to go.

DEAR JONES: Yes. [*An unholy toot from the steam whistle.*] And there he is signalling that yacht to take us off!

BABY VAN RENSSELAER: I must go to my aunt now.

DEAR JONES: Why — there's no hurry.

BABY VAN RENSSELAER: No, but she'll be so frightened — she'll think it's going to blow up or something.

Baby Van Rensselaer disappeared in the depths of the cabin. Dear Jones disconsolately walked the deck in solitary silence for five minutes. When Baby Van Rensselaer reappeared, his spirits rose.

BABY VAN RENSSELAER: My aunt is afraid you may have difficulty in reaching New London to-night. She wants me to ask you if you won't stay over-night at her place at Watch Hill?

DEAR JONES: Won't I? Well, I will — have much pleasure in accepting your aunt's invitation.

VI.

THE SIXTH CONVERSATION.

TUESDAY, September 5, 1882. (Evening.)

A row of Japanese lanterns shed a Cathayan light along the little path leading from the Duchess's house on a rocky promontory to the little beach which nestled under its shoulder. The moon softly and judiciously lit up the baby breakers which in Long Island Sound imitate the surf of the outer sea. It threw eerie shadows behind the bath-houses, and fell with gentle radiance upon two dripping but shapely figures emerging from the water, where the other bathers were unwisely lingering.

DEAR JONES: I think this is simply delightful. I really never got the perfect enjoyment of an evening swim before.

BABY VAN RENSSELAER: I am glad you enjoyed it.

DEAR JONES: There is something so charming in this aristocratic seclusion, with the shouts and laughter of the vulgar herd just far enough off to be picturesque — if you can call a noise picturesque.

BABY VAN RENSSELAER [*coldly*]: I think this beach might be a little more private — it's shared in common by these three cottages.

DEAR JONES: But they seem to be very nice people here. And they all swim so well, it quite put me on my mettle. You are really a splendid swimmer, do you know it? And that girl I towed out to the buoy, who is she?

BABY VAN RENSSELAER [*explosively*]: Mr. Jones, this is positively insulting!

DEAR JONES: Wh — what — wh — why? I don't understand you.

BABY VAN RENSSELAER: To pretend that you don't know that Hitchcock woman!

DEAR JONES [*innocently*]: Was that Miss Hitchcock? I did n't recognize her.

BABY VAN RENSSELAER: If this is your idea of humor, Mr. Jones, it is simply offensive!

DEAR JONES: But, upon my soul, I did n't know the girl — nor she me!

BABY VAN RENSSELAER: You did n't know her? After you have been staying two weeks at her house at Newport?

DEAR JONES [*with something like dignity*]: I was staying at her father's house, Miss Van Rensselaer, and Miss Hitchcock was away on a visit.

BABY VAN RENSSELAER: Up the Saguenay, perhaps?

DEAR JONES: Very likely. Miss Hitchcock may have left a large part of the Saguenay unexplored for all I know. I was introduced to her party only half an hour before we got off the boat at Quebec.

BABY VAN RENSSELAER: Long enough, however, to discover that she was "bright."

DEAR JONES: Quite long enough, Miss Van Rensselaer. One may find out a great deal of another's character in half an hour.

There was a pause, which was filled by the strains of a Virginia reel, coming from one of the cottages high up on the bank, where an impromptu dance was just begun. The moonlight fell on Baby Van Rensselaer's little white teeth, set firmly between her parted lips. The pause was broken.

BABY VAN RENSSELAER: If you propose to descend to brutality of this sort, Mr. Jones, I think we need prolong neither the conversation — nor the acquaintance.

DEAR JONES [*honestly*]: No — you can't mean that — Miss Van Rensselaer — Baby —

BABY VAN RENSSELAER: What, sir! Your familiarity is — I can't stand familiarity from you! (*She clenches her little hands.*)

DEAR JONES: You have no right to treat me like this. If I am familiar it is because I love you — and you know it!

BABY VAN RENSSELAER: This is the first I have heard of it, sir. I trust it will be the last. Will you kindly permit me to pass, or must I —

DEAR JONES: You may go where you wish, Miss Van Renssellaer — No, come, this is ridiculous —

BABY VAN RENSSELAER: Is it?

Dear Jones: I mean it is foolish. Don't let us —

Baby Van Rensselaer: Don't let us see each other again!

VII.

THE SEVENTH CONVERSATION.

Thursday, February 14, 1884.

As the soft, low notes of the wedding-march from "Lohengrin" fell gently from the organ-loft over the entrance of Grace Church, the quartet of able-bodied ushers passed up the centre aisle and parted the white ribbons—a silken barrier which they had gallantly defended for an hour in a vain effort to keep the common herd of acquaintance separate from the chosen many of the family. Behind them came two pretty little girls, strewing the aisle with white flowers from their aprons. The four bridesmaids, two abreast, passed up the aisle after the little girls, proud in their reflected glory. Then came the bride, leaning on Judge Gillespie's arm, and radiant with youth and beauty and happiness. As the procession drew near the chancel-rail, the groom came from the vestry and advanced to meet her, accompanied by his best man, Uncle Larry, who relieved him of his hat and overcoat, the which he would dextrously return to him when the happy couple should leave the church man and wife. And in due time the Bishop asked, "Wilt thou have this Woman to thy wedded wife?"

Dear Jones: I will.

The Bishop asked again, "Wilt thou have this Man to thy wedded husband?"

Baby Van Rensselaer: I will.

As they knelt at the altar the sun came out and fell through the window, and the stained glass sifted down on them the mingled hues of hope and of faith and love; and the Bishop blessed them.

THE RIVAL GHOSTS.

BY BRANDER MATTHEWS.

THE good ship sped on her way across the calm Atlantic. It was an outward passage, according to the little charts which the company had charily distributed, but most of the passengers were homeward bound, after a summer of rest and recreation, and they were counting the days before they might hope to see Fire Island Light. On the lee side of the boat, comfortably sheltered from the wind, and just by the door of the captain's room (which was theirs during the day), sat a little group of returning Americans. The Duchess (she was down on the the purser's list as Mrs. Martin, but her friends and familiars called her the Duchess of Washington Square) and Baby Van Rensselaer (she was quite old enough to vote, had her sex been entitled to that duty, but as the younger of two sisters she was still the baby of the family) — the Duchess and Baby Van Rensselaer were discussing the pleasant English voice and the not unpleasant English accent of a manly young lordling who was going to America for sport. Uncle Larry and Dear Jones were enticing each other into a bet on the ship's run of the morrow.

"I'll give you two to one she don't make 420," said Dear Jones.

"I'll take it," answered Uncle Larry. "We made 427 the fifth day last year." It was Uncle Larry's seventeenth visit to Europe, and this was therefore his thirty-fourth voyage.

"And when did you get in?" asked Baby Van Rensselaer. "I don't care a bit about the run, so long as we get in soon."

"We crossed the bar Sunday night, just seven days after we left Queenstown, and we dropped anchor off Quarantine at three o'clock on Monday morning."

"I hope we sha' n't do that this time. I can't seem to sleep any when the boat stops."

"I can; but I did n't," continued Uncle Larry; "because my stateroom was the most for'ard in the boat, and the donkey-engine that let down the anchor was right over my head."

"So you got up and saw the sunrise over the bay," said Dear Jones, "with the electric lights of the city twinkling in the distance, and the first faint flush of the dawn in the east just over Fort Lafayette, and the rosy tinge which spread softly upward, and"—

"Did you both come back together?" asked the Duchess.

"Because he has crossed thirty-four times you must not suppose he has a monopoly in sunrises," retorted Dear Jones. "No; this was my own sunrise; and a mighty pretty one it was, too."

"I'm not matching sunrises with you," remarked Uncle Larry calmly; "but I'm willing to back a merry

jest called forth by my sunrise against any two merry
jests called forth by yours."

"I confess reluctantly that my sunrise evoked no
merry jest at all." Dear Jones was an honest man,
and would scorn to invent a merry jest on the spur of
the moment.

"That's where my sunrise has the call," said Uncle
Larry complacently.

"What was the merry jest?" was Baby Van Rensselaer's inquiry, the natural result of a feminine curiosity
thus artistically excited.

"Well, here it is. I was standing aft, near a patriotic American and a wandering Irishman, and the
patriotic American rashly declared that you couldn't
see a sunrise like that anywhere in Europe, and this
gave the Irishman his chance, and he said, 'Sure ye
don't have 'm here till we're through with 'em over
there.'"

"It is true," said Dear Jones thoughtfully, "that
they do have some things over there better than we do;
for instance, umbrellas."

"And gowns," added the Duchess.

"And antiquities"— this was Uncle Larry's contribution.

"And we do have some things so much better in
America!" protested Baby Van Rensselaer, as yet
uncorrupted by any worship of the effete monarchies
of despotic Europe. "We make lots of things a great
deal nicer than you can get them in Europe — especially ice-cream."

"And pretty girls," added Dear Jones; but he did
not look at her.

" And spooks," remarked Uncle Larry casually.

"Spooks?" queried the Duchess.

"Spooks. I maintain the word. Ghosts, if you like that better, or spectres. We turn out the best quality of spook "—

" You forget the lovely ghost stories about the Rhine, and the Black Forest," interrupted Miss Van Rensselaer, with feminine inconsistency.

"I remember the Rhine and the Black Forest and all the other haunts of elves and fairies and hobgoblins; but for good honest spooks there is no place like home. And what differentiates our spook — *spiritus Americanus* — from the ordinary ghost of literature is that it responds to the American sense of humor. Take Irving's stories, for example. *The Headless Horseman*, that's a comic ghost story. And Rip Van Winkle — consider what humor, and what good-humor, there is in the telling of his meeting with the goblin crew of Hendrik Hudson's men ! A still better example of this American way of dealing with legend and mystery is the marvellous tale of the rival ghosts."

" The rival ghosts?" queried the Duchess and Baby Van Rensselaer together. " Who were they?"

" Did n't I ever tell you about them?" answered Uncle Larry, a gleam of approaching joy flashing from his eye.

" Since he is bound to tell us sooner or later, we'd better be resigned, and hear it now," said Dear Jones.

" If you are not more eager, I won't tell it at all."

" Oh, do, Uncle Larry; you know I just dote on ghost stories," pleaded Baby Van Rensselaer.

"Once upon a time," began Uncle Larry — "in fact, a very few years ago — there lived in the thriving town of New York a young American called Duncan — Eliphalet Duncan. Like his name, he was half Yankee and half Scotch, and naturally he was a lawyer, and had come to New York to make his way. His father was a Scotchman, who had come over and settled in Boston, and married a Salem girl. When Eliphalet Duncan was about twenty he lost both of his parents. His father left him with enough money to give him a start, and a strong feeling of pride in his Scotch birth; you see there was a title in the family in Scotland, and although Eliphalet's father was the younger son of a younger son, yet he always remembered, and always bade his only son to remember, that his ancestry was noble. His mother left him her full share of Yankee grit, and a little old house in Salem which had belonged to her family for more than two hundred years. She was a Hitchcock, and the Hitchcocks had been settled in Salem since the year 1. It was a great-great-grandfather of Mr. Eliphalet Hitchcock who was foremost in the time of the Salem witchcraft craze. And this little old house which she left to my friend Eliphalet Duncan was haunted."

"By the ghost of one of the witches, of course," interrupted Dear Jones.

"Now how could it be the ghost of a witch, since the witches were all burned at the stake? You never heard of anybody who was burned having a ghost, did you?"

"That's an argument in favor of cremation, at

any rate," replied Jones, evading the direct question.

"It is, if you don't like ghosts. I do," said Baby Van Rensselaer.

"And so do I," added Uncle Larry. "I love a ghost as dearly as an Englishman loves a lord."

"Go on with your story," said the Duchess, majestically overruling all extraneous discussion.

"This little old house at Salem was haunted," resumed Uncle Larry. "And by a very distinguished ghost — or at least by a ghost with very remarkable attributes."

"What was he like?" asked Baby Van Rensselaer, with a premonitory shiver of anticipatory delight.

"It had a lot of peculiarities. In the first place, it never appeared to the master of the house. Mostly it confined its visitations to unwelcome guests. In the course of the last hundred years it had frightened away four successive mothers-in-law, while never intruding on the head of the household."

"I guess that ghost had been one of the boys when he was alive and in the flesh." This was Dear Jones's contribution to the telling of the tale.

"In the second place," continued Uncle Larry, "it never frightened anybody the first time it appeared. Only on the second visit were the ghost-seers scared; but then they were scared enough for twice, and they rarely mustered up courage enough to risk a third interview. One of the most curious characteristics of this well-meaning spook was that it had no face — or at least that nobody ever saw its face."

"Perhaps he kept his countenance veiled?" queried the Duchess, who was beginning to remember that she never did like ghost stories.

"That was what I was never able to find out. I have asked several people who saw the ghost, and none of them could tell me anything about its face, and yet while in its presence they never noticed its features, and never remarked on their absence or concealment. It was only afterward when they tried to recall calmly all the circumstances of meeting with the mysterious stranger, that they became aware that they had not seen its face. And they could not say whether the features were covered, or whether they were wanting, or what the trouble was. They knew only that the face was never seen. And no matter how often they might see it, they never fathomed this mystery. To this day nobody knows whether the ghost which used to haunt the little old house in Salem had a face, or what manner of face it had."

"How awfully weird!" said Baby Van Rensselaer. "And why did the ghost go away?"

"I have n't said it went away," answered Uncle Larry, with much dignity.

"But you said it *used* to haunt the little old house at Salem, so I supposed it had moved. Did n't it?"

"You shall be told in due time. Eliphalet Duncan used to spend most of his summer vacations at Salem, and the ghost never bothered him at all, for he was the master of the house — much to his disgust, too, because he wanted to see for himself the mysterious tenant at will of his property. But he never saw it,

never. He arranged with friends to call him whenever it might appear, and he slept in the next room
with the door open; and yet when their frightened
cries waked him the ghost was gone, and his only
reward was to hear reproachful sighs as soon as he
went back to bed. You see, the ghost thought it was
not fair of Eliphalet to seek an introduction which was
plainly unwelcome."

Dear Jones interrupted the story-teller by getting up
and tucking a heavy rug more snugly around Baby Van
Rensselaer's feet, for the sky was now overcast and
gray, and the air was damp and penetrating.

"One fine spring morning," pursued Uncle Larry,
"Eliphalet Duncan received great news. I told you
that there was a title in the family in Scotland, and
that Eliphalet's father was the younger son of a younger
son. Well, it happened that all Eliphalet's father's
brothers and uncles had died off without male issue
except the eldest son of the eldest, and he, of course,
bore the title, and was Baron Duncan of Duncan.
Now the great news that Eliphalet Duncan received
in New York one fine spring morning was that Baron
Duncan and his only son had been yachting in the
Hebrides, and they had been caught in a black squall,
and they were both dead. So my friend Eliphalet
Duncan inherited the title and the estates."

"How romantic!" said the Duchess. "So he was
a baron!"

"Well," answered Uncle Larry, "he was a baron if
he chose. But he did n't choose."

"More fool he!" said Dear Jones sententiously.

" Well," answered Uncle Larry, " I 'm not so sure of that. You see, Eliphalet Duncan was half Scotch and half Yankee, and he had two eyes to the main chance. He held his tongue about his windfall of luck until he could find out whether the Scotch estates were enough to keep up the Scotch title. He soon discovered that they were not, and that the late Lord Duncan, having married money, kept up such state as he could out of the revenues of the dowry of Lady Duncan. And Eliphalet, he decided that he would rather be a well-fed lawyer in New York, living comfortably on his practice, than a starving lord in Scotland, living scantily on his title."

" But he kept his title ? " asked the Duchess.

" Well," answered Uncle Larry, " he kept it quiet. I knew it, and a friend or two more. But Eliphalet was a sight too smart to put Baron Duncan of Duncan, Attorney and Counsellor at Law, on his shingle."

" What has all this got to do with your ghost ? " asked Dear Jones pertinently.

" Nothing with that ghost, but a good deal with another ghost. Eliphalet was very learned in spirit lore — perhaps because he owned the haunted house at Salem, perhaps because he was a Scotchman by descent. At all events, he had made a special study of the wraiths and white ladies and banshees and bogies of all kinds whose sayings and doings and warnings are recorded in the annals of the Scottish nobility. In fact, he was acquainted with the habits of every reputable spook in the Scotch peerage. And he knew that there was a Duncan ghost attached to the per-

son of the holder of the title of Baron Duncan of
Duncan."

"So, besides being the owner of a haunted house in
Salem, he was also a haunted man in Scotland?" asked
Baby Van Rensselaer.

"Just so. But the Scotch ghost was not unpleasant,
like the Salem ghost, although it had one peculiarity in
common with its transatlantic fellow-spook. It never
appeared to the holder of the title, just as the other
never was visible to the owner of the house. In fact,
the Duncan ghost was never seen at all. It was a
guardian angel only. Its sole duty was to be in personal attendance on Baron Duncan of Duncan, and to
warn him of impending evil. The traditions of the
house told that the Barons of Duncan had again and
again felt a premonition of ill fortune. Some of them
had yielded and withdrawn from the venture they
had undertaken, and it had failed dismally. Some had
been obstinate, and had hardened their hearts, and had
gone on reckless to defeat and to death. In no case
had a Lord Duncan been exposed to peril without fair
warning."

"Then how came it that the father and son were
lost in the yacht off the Hebrides?" asked Dear
Jones.

"Because they were too enlightened to yield to
superstition. There is extant now a letter of Lord
Duncan, written to his wife a few minutes before he
and his son set sail, in which he tells her how hard he
has had to struggle with an almost overmastering desire to give up the trip. Had he obeyed the friendly

warning of the family ghost, the latter would have been spared a journey across the Atlantic."

" Did the ghost leave Scotland for America as soon as the old baron died?" asked Baby Van Rensselaer, with much interest.

"How did he come over," queried Dear Jones — " in the steerage, or as a cabin passenger?"

"I don't know," answered Uncle Larry calmly, " and Eliphalet, he didn't know. For as he was in no danger, and stood in no need of warning, he couldn't tell whether the ghost was on duty or not. Of course he was on the watch for it all the time. But he never got any proof of its presence until he went down to the little old house of Salem, just before the Fourth of July. He took a friend down with him — a young fellow who had been in the regular army since the day Fort Sumter was fired on, and who thought that after four years of the little unpleasantness down South, including six months in Libby, and after ten years of fighting the bad Indians on the plains, he wasn't likely to be much frightened by a ghost. Well, Eliphalet and the officer sat out on the porch all the evening smoking and talking over points in military law. A little after twelve o'clock, just as they began to think it was about time to turn in, they heard the most ghastly noise in the house. It wasn't a shriek, or a howl, or a yell, or anything they could put a name to. It was an undeterminate, inexplicable shiver and shudder of sound, which went wailing out of the window. The officer had been at Cold Harbor, but he felt himself getting colder this time. Eliphalet knew it was the ghost who haunted the house. As this weird sound died away, it was followed by another, sharp, short, blood-curdling in its intensity. Something in this cry seemed familiar to Eliphalet, and he felt sure that it proceeded from the family ghost, the warning wraith of the Duncans."

"Do I understand you to intimate that both ghosts were there together?" inquired the Duchess anxiously.

"Both of them were there," answered Uncle Larry. "You see, one of them belonged to the house, and had to be there all the time, and the other was attached to the person of Baron Duncan, and had to follow him there; wherever he was, there was that ghost also. But Eliphalet, he had scarcely time to think this out when he heard both sounds again, not one after another, but both together, and something told him — some sort of an instinct he had — that those two ghosts did n't agree, did n't get on together, did n't exactly hit it off; in fact, that they were quarrelling."

"Quarrelling ghosts! Well, I never!" was Baby Van Rensselaer's remark.

"It is a blessed thing to see ghosts dwell together in unity," said Dear Jones.

And the Duchess added, "It would certainly be setting a better example."

"You know," resumed Uncle Larry, "that two waves of light or of sound may interfere and produce darkness or silence. So it was with these rival spooks. They interfered, but they did not produce silence or darkness. On the contrary, as soon as Eliphalet and the officer went into the house, there began at once a series of spiritualistic manifestations, a regular dark séance. A tambourine was played upon, a bell was rung, and a flaming banjo went singing around the room."

"Where did they get the banjo?" asked Dear Jones skeptically.

"I don't know. Materialized it, maybe, just as they did the tambourine. You don't suppose a quiet New York lawyer kept a stock of musical instruments large enough to fit out a strolling minstrel troupe just on the chance of a pair of ghosts coming to give him a surprise party, do you? Every spook has its own instrument of torture. Angels play on harps, I'm informed, and spirits delight in banjos and tambourines. These spooks of Eliphalet Duncan's were ghosts with all the modern improvements, and I guess they were capable of providing their own musical weapons. At all events, they had them there in the little old house at Salem the night Eliphalet and his friend came down. And they played on them, and they rang the bell, and they rapped here, there, and everywhere. And they kept it up all night."

"All night?" asked the awe-stricken Duchess.

"All night long," said Uncle Larry solemnly; "and the next night, too. Eliphalet did not get a wink of sleep, neither did his friend. On the second night the house ghost was seen by the officer; on the third night it showed itself again; and the next morning the officer packed his grip-sack and took the first train to Boston. He was a New Yorker, but he said he'd sooner go to Boston than see that ghost again. Eliphalet, he wasn't scared at all, partly because he never saw either the domiciliary or the titular spook, and partly because he felt himself on friendly terms with the spirit world, and did n't scare easily. But after losing three nights' sleep and the society of his friend, he began to be a little impatient, and to think that the thing had gone far enough. You see, while in a way he was fond of ghosts, yet he liked them best one at a time. Two ghosts were one too many. He was n't bent on making a collection of spooks. He and one ghost were company, but he and two ghosts were a crowd."

"What did he do?" asked Baby Van Rensselaer.

"Well, he could n't do anything. He waited awhile, hoping they would get tired; but he got tired out first. You see, it comes natural to a spook to sleep in the daytime, but a man wants to sleep nights, and they would n't let him sleep nights. They kept on wrangling and quarrelling incessantly; they manifested and they dark-séanced as regularly as the old clock on the stairs struck twelve; they rapped and they rang bells and they banged the tambourine and they threw the flaming banjo about the house, and, worse than all, they swore."

"I did not know that spirits were addicted to bad language," said the Duchess.

"How did he know they were swearing? Could he hear them?" asked Dear Jones.

"That was just it," responded Uncle Larry; "he could not hear them — at least not distinctly. There were inarticulate murmurs and stifled rumblings. But the impression produced on him was that they were swearing. If they had only sworn right out, he would not have minded it so much, because he would have known the worst. But the feeling that the air was full of suppressed profanity was very wearing, and after standing it for a week, he gave up in disgust and went to the White Mountains."

"Leaving them to fight it out, I suppose," interjected Baby Van Rensselaer.

"Not at all," explained Uncle Larry. "They could not quarrel unless he was present. You see, he could not leave the titular ghost behind him, and the domiciliary ghost could not leave the house. When he went away he took the family ghost with him, leaving the house ghost behind. Now spooks can't quarrel when they are a hundred miles apart any more than men can."

"And what happened afterward?" asked Baby Van Rensselaer, with a pretty impatience.

"A most marvellous thing happened. Eliphalet Duncan went to the White Mountains, and in the car of the railroad that runs to the top of Mount Washington he met a classmate whom he had not seen for years, and this classmate introduced Duncan to his sister, and this sister was a remarkably pretty girl, and Duncan fell in love with her at first sight, and by the time he got to the top of Mount Washington he was so deep in love that he began to consider his own unworthiness, and to wonder whether she might ever be induced to care for him a little — ever so little."

"I don't think that is so marvellous a thing," said Dear Jones, glancing at Baby Van Rensselaer.

"Who was she?" asked the Duchess, who had once lived in Philadelphia.

"She was Miss Kitty Sutton, of San Francisco, and she was a daughter of old Judge Sutton, of the firm of Pixley and Sutton."

"A very respectable family," assented the Duchess.

"I hope she wasn't a daughter of that loud and vulgar old Mrs. Sutton whom I met at Saratoga, one summer, four or five years ago?" said Dear Jones.

"Probably she was."

"She was a horrid old woman. The boys used to call her Mother Gorgon."

"The pretty Kitty Sutton with whom Eliphalet Duncan had fallen in love was the daughter of Mother Gorgon. But he never saw the mother, who was in 'Frisco, or Los Angeles, or Santa Fé, or somewhere out West, and he saw a great deal of the daughter, who was up in the White Mountains. She was travelling with her brother and his wife, and as they journeyed from hotel to hotel, Duncan went with them, and filled out the quartette. Before the end of the summer he began to think about proposing. Of course he had lots of chances, going on excursions as they were every day. He made up his mind to seize the first opportunity, and that very evening he took her out for a moonlight row on Lake Winnipiseogee. As he handed her into the boat he resolved to do it, and he had a glimmer of a suspicion that she knew he was going to do it, too."

"Girls," said Dear Jones, "never go out in a rowboat at night with a young man unless you mean to accept him."

"Sometimes it's best to refuse him, and get it over once for all," said Baby Van Rensselaer.

"As Eliphalet took the oars he felt a sudden chill. He tried to shake it off, but in vain. He began to have a growing consciousness of impending evil. Before he had taken ten strokes — and he was a swift oarsman — he was aware of a mysterious presence between him and Miss Sutton."

"Was it the guardian-angel ghost warning him off the match?" interrupted Dear Jones.

"That's just what it was," said Uncle Larry. "And he yielded to it, and kept his peace, and rowed Miss Sutton back to the hotel with his proposal unspoken."

"More fool he," said Dear Jones. "It will take more than one ghost to keep me from proposing when my mind is made up." And he looked at Baby Van Rensselaer.

"The next morning," continued Uncle Larry, "Eliphalet overslept himself, and when he went down to a late breakfast he found that the Suttons had gone to New York by the morning train. He wanted to follow them at once, and again he felt the mysterious presence overpowering his will. He struggled two days, and at last he roused himself to do what he wanted in spite of the spook. When he arrived in New York it was late in the evening. He dressed himself hastily, and went to the hotel where the Suttons put up, in the hope of seeing at least her brother. The guardian angel fought every inch of the walk with him, until he began to wonder whether, if Miss Sutton were to take him, the spook would forbid the banns. At the hotel he saw no one that night, and he went home determined to call as early as he could the next afternoon, and make an end of it. When he left his office about two o'clock the next day to learn his fate, he had not walked five blocks before he discovered that the wraith of the Duncans had withdrawn his opposition to the suit. There was no feeling of impending evil, no resistance, no struggle, no consciousness of an opposing presence. Eliphalet was greatly encouraged. He walked briskly to the hotel; he found Miss Sutton alone. He asked her the question, and got his answer."

"She accepted him, of course," said Baby Van Rensselaer.

"Of course," said Uncle Larry. "And while they were in the first flush of joy, swapping confidences and confessions, her brother came into the parlor with an expression of pain on his face and a telegram in his hand. The former was caused by the latter, which was from 'Frisco, and which announced the sudden death of Mrs. Sutton, their mother."

"And that was why the ghost no longer opposed the match?" questioned Dear Jones.

"Exactly. You see, the family ghost knew that Mother Gorgon was an awful obstacle to Duncan's happiness, so it warned him. But the moment the obstacle was removed, it gave its consent at once."

The fog was lowering its thick damp curtain, and it was beginning to be difficult to see from one end of the boat to the other. Dear Jones tightened the rug which enwrapped Baby Van Rensselaer, and then withdrew again into his own substantial coverings.

Uncle Larry paused in his story long enough to light another of the tiny cigars he always smoked.

"I infer that Lord Duncan"— the Duchess was scrupulous in the bestowal of titles — "saw no more of the ghosts after he was married."

"He never saw them at all, at any time, either before or since. But they came very near breaking off the match, and thus breaking two young hearts."

"You don't mean to say that they knew any just cause or impediment why they should not forever after hold their peace?" asked Dear Jones.

"How could a ghost, or even two ghosts, keep a girl from marrying the man she loved?" This was Baby Van Rensselaer's question.

"It seems curious, does n't it?" and Uncle Larry tried to warm himself by two or three sharp pulls at his fiery little cigar. "And the circumstances are quite as curious as the fact itself. You see, Miss Sutton would n't be married for a year after her mother's death, so she and Duncan had lots of time to tell each other all they knew. Eliphalet, he got to know a good deal about the girls she went to school with, and Kitty, she learned all about his family. He did n't tell her about the title for a long time, as he was n't one to brag. But he described to her the little old house at Salem. And one evening toward the end of the summer, the wedding-day having been appointed for early in September, she told him that she did n't want a

bridal tour at all; she just wanted to go down to the
little old house at Salem to spend her honeymoon in
peace and quiet, with nothing to do and nobody to
bother them. Well, Eliphalet jumped at the suggestion: it suited him down to the ground. All of a sudden he remembered the spooks, and it knocked him all
of a heap. He had told her about the Duncan banshee,
and the idea of having an ancestral ghost in personal
attendance on her husband tickled her immensely.
But he had never said anything about the ghost which
haunted the little old house at Salem. He knew she
would be frightened out of her wits if the house ghost
revealed itself to her, and he saw at once that it would
be impossible to go to Salem on their wedding trip.
So he told her all about it, and how whenever he went
to Salem the two ghosts interfered, and gave dark
séances and manifested and materialized and made the
place absolutely impossible. Kitty, she listened in
silence, and Eliphalet, he thought she had changed her
mind. But she had n't done anything of the kind."

"Just like a man — to think she was going to," remarked Baby Van Rensselaer.

"She just told him she could not bear ghosts herself,
but she would not marry a man who was afraid of
them."

"Just like a girl — to be so inconsistent," remarked
Dear Jones.

Uncle Larry's tiny cigar had long been extinct. He
lighted a new one, and continued: "Eliphalet protested in vain. Kitty said her mind was made up.
She was determined to pass her honeymoon in the

little old house at Salem, and she was equally determined not to go there as long as there were any ghosts
there.   Until he could assure her that the spectral tenant had received notice to quit, and that there was no
danger of manifestations and materializing, she refused
to be married at all.   She did not intend to have her
honeymoon interrupted by two wrangling ghosts, and
the wedding could be postponed until he had made
ready the house for her."

"She was an unreasonable young woman," said the
Duchess.

"Well, that's what Eliphalet thought, much as he
was in love with her.   And he believed he could talk
her out of her determination.   But he couldn't.   She
was set.   And when a girl is set, there's nothing to do
but to yield to the inevitable.   And that's just what
Eliphalet did.   He saw he would either have to give
her up or to get the ghosts out; and as he loved her
and did not care for the ghosts, he resolved to tackle
the ghosts.   He had clear grit, Eliphalet had — he was
half Scotch and half Yankee, and neither breed turns
tail in a hurry.   So he made his plans and he went
down to Salem.   As he said good-by to Kitty he had
an impression that she was sorry she had made him go,
but she kept up bravely, and put a bold face on it, and
saw him off, and went home and cried for an hour, and
was perfectly miserable until he came back the next
day."

"Did he succeed in driving the ghosts away?"
asked Baby Van Rensselaer, with great interest.

"That's just what I'm coming to," said Uncle

Larry, pausing at the critical moment, in the manner of the trained story-teller. "You see, Eliphalet had got a rather tough job, and he would gladly have had an extension of time on the contract, but he had to choose between the girl and the ghosts, and he wanted the girl. He tried to invent or remember some short and easy way with ghosts, but he couldn't. He wished that somebody had invented a specific for spooks — something that would make the ghosts come out of the house and die in the yard. He wondered if he could not tempt the ghosts to run in debt, so that he might get the sheriff to help him. He wondered also whether the ghosts could not be overcome with strong drink — a dissipated spook, a spook with delirium tremens, might be committed to the inebriate asylum. But none of these things seemed feasible."

"What did he do?" interrupted Dear Jones. "The learned counsel will please speak to the point."

"You will regret this unseemly haste," said Uncle Larry, gravely, "when you know what really happened.

"What was it, Uncle Larry?" asked Baby Van Rensselaer. "I'm all impatience."

And Uncle Larry proceeded:

"Eliphalet went down to the little old house at Salem, and as soon as the clock struck twelve the rival ghosts began wrangling as before. Raps here, there, and everywhere, ringing bells, banging tambourines, strumming banjos sailing about the room, and all the other manifestations and materializations followed one another just as they had the summer before. The only difference Eliphalet could detect was a stronger flavor in the spectral profanity; and this, of course, was only a vague impression, for he did not actually hear a single word. He waited awhile in patience, listening and watching. Of course he never saw either of the ghosts, because neither of them could appear to him. At last he got his dander up, and he thought it was about time to interfere, so he rapped on the table, and asked for silence. As soon as he felt that the spooks were listening to him he explained the situation to them. He told them he was in love, and that he could not marry unless they vacated the house. He appealed to them as old friends, and he laid claim to their gratitude. The titular ghost had been sheltered by the Duncan family for hundreds of years, and the domiciliary ghost had had free lodging in the little old house at Salem for nearly two centuries. He implored them to settle their differences, and to get him out of his difficulty at once. He suggested that they had better fight it out then and there, and see who was master. He had brought down with him all needful weapons. And he pulled out his valise, and spread on the table a pair of navy revolvers, a pair of shot-guns, a pair of duelling swords, and a couple of bowie-knives. He offered to serve as second for both parties, and to give the word when to begin. He also took out of his valise a pack of cards and a bottle of poison, telling them that if they wished to avoid carnage they might cut the cards to see which one should take the poison. Then he waited anxiously for their reply. For a little space there was silence. Then he became conscious of a tremulous shivering in one corner of the room, and he remembered that he had heard from that direction what sounded like a frightened sigh when he made the first suggestion of the duel. Something told him that this was the domiciliary ghost, and that it was badly scared. Then he was impressed by a certain movement in the opposite corner of the room, as though the titular ghost were drawing himself up with offended dignity. Eliphalet could n't exactly see these things, because he never saw the ghosts, but he felt them. After a silence of nearly a minute a voice came from the corner where the family ghost stood — a voice strong and full, but trembling slightly with suppressed passion. And this voice told Eliphalet it was plain enough that he had not long been the head of the Duncans, and that he had never properly considered the characteristics of his race if now he supposed that one of his blood could draw his sword against a woman. Eliphalet said he had never suggested that the Duncan ghost should raise his hand against a woman, and all he wanted was that the Duncan ghost should fight the other ghost. And then the voice told Eliphalet that the other ghost was a woman."

"What?" said Dear Jones, sitting up suddenly. "You don't mean to tell me that the ghost which haunted the house was a woman?"

"Those were the very words Eliphalet Duncan used," said Uncle Larry; "but he did not need to wait for the answer. All at once he recalled the traditions about the domiciliary ghost, and he knew that what the titular ghost said was the fact. He had never thought of the sex of a spook, but there was no doubt

whatever that the house ghost was a woman. No
sooner was this firmly fixed in Eliphalet's mind than
he saw his way out of the difficulty. The ghosts must
be married!—for then there would be no more inter-
ference, no more quarrelling, no more manifestations
and materializations, no more dark séances, with their
raps and bells and tambourines and banjos. At first
the ghosts would not hear of it. The voice in the corner declared that the Duncan wraith had never thought
of matrimony. But Eliphalet argued with them, and
pleaded and persuaded and coaxed, and dwelt on the
advantages of matrimony. He had to confess, of
course, that he did not know how to get a clergyman
to marry them; but the voice from the corner gravely
told him that there need be no difficulty in regard to
that, as there was no lack of spiritual chaplains. Then,
for the first time, the house ghost spoke, in a low, clear,
gentle voice, and with a quaint, old-fashioned New
England accent, which contrasted sharply with the
broad Scotch speech of the family ghost. She said
that Eliphalet Duncan seemed to have forgotten that
she was married. But this did not upset Eliphalet at
all; he remembered the whole case clearly, and he told
her she was not a married ghost, but a widow, since
her husband had been hung for murdering her. Then
the Duncan ghost drew attention to the great disparity
in their ages, saying that he was nearly four hundred
and fifty years old, while she was barely two hundred.
But Eliphalet had not talked to juries for nothing; he
just buckled to, and coaxed those ghosts into matrimony. Afterward he came to the conclusion that they

were willing to be coaxed, but at the time he thought he had pretty hard work to convince them of the advantages of the plan."

"Did he succeed?" asked Baby Van Rensselaer, with a young lady's interest in matrimony.

"He did," said Uncle Larry. "He talked the wraith of the Duncans and the spectre of the little old house at Salem into a matrimonial engagement. And from the time they were engaged he had no more trouble with them. They were rival ghosts no longer. They were married by their spiritual chaplain the very same day that Eliphalet Duncan met Kitty Sutton in front of the railing of Grace Church. The ghostly bride and bridegroom went away at once on their bridal tour, and Lord and Lady Duncan went down to the little old house at Salem to pass their honeymoon."

Uncle Larry stopped. His tiny cigar was out again. The tale of the rival ghosts was told. A solemn silence fell on the little party on the deck of the ocean steamer, broken harshly by the hoarse roar of the fog-horn.

A LETTER AND A PARAGRAPH.

BY H. C. BUNNER.

I.

THE LETTER.

NEW YORK, Nov. 16, 1883.

MY DEAR WILL: —

You cannot be expected to remember it, but this is the fifth anniversary of my wedding-day, and to-morrow — it will be to-morrow before this letter is closed — is my birthday — my fortieth. My head is full of those thoughts which the habit of my life moves me to put on paper, where I can best express them; and yet which must be written for only the friendliest of eyes. It is not the least of my happiness in this life that I have one friend to whom I can unlock my heart as I can to you.

The wife has just been putting your namesake to sleep. Don't infer that, even on the occasion of this family feast, he has been allowed to sit up until half past eleven. He went to bed properly enough, with a tear or two, at eight; but when his mother stole into his room just now, after her custom, I heard his small voice raised in drowsy inquiry; and I followed her, and slipped the curtain of the doorway aside, and looked. But I did not go into the room.

The shaded lamp was making a yellow glory in one spot — the head of the little brass crib where my wife knelt by my boy. I saw the little face, so like hers, turned up to her. There was a smile on it that I knew was a reflection of hers. He was winking in a merry half-attempt to keep awake; but wakefulness was slipping away from him under the charm of that smile that I could not see. His brown eyes closed, and opened for an instant, and closed again as the tender, happy hush of a child's sleep settled down upon him, and he was gone where we in our heavier slumbers shall hardly follow him. Then, before I could see my wife's face as she bent and kissed him, I let the curtain fall, and crept back here, to sit by the last of the fire, and see that sacred sight again with the spiritual eyes, and to dream wonderingly over the unspeakable happiness that has in some mysterious way come to me, undeserving.

I tell you, Will, that moment was to me like one of those moments of waking that we know in childhood, when we catch the going of a dream too subtly sweet to belong to this earth — a glad vision, gone before our eyes can open wide; not to be figured into any earthly idea, leaving in its passage a joy so high and fine that the poets tell us it is a memory of some heaven from which our young souls are yet fresh.

You can understand how it is that I find it hard to realize that there can be such things in my life; for you know what that life was up to a few years ago. I am like a man who has spent his first thirty years in a cave. It takes more than a decade above ground to make him quite believe in the sun and the blue of the sky.

I was sitting just now before the hearth, with my feet in the bearskin rug you sent us two Christmases ago. The light of the low wood fire was chasing the shadows around the room, over my books and my pictures, and all the fine and gracious luxuries with which I may now make my eyes and my heart glad, and pamper the tastes that grow with feeding. I was taking count, so to speak, of my prosperity — the material treasures, the better treasure that I find in such portion of fame as the world has allotted me, and the treasure of treasures across the threshold of the next room — in the next room? No — there, here, in every room, in every corner of the house, filling it with peace, is the gentle and holy spirit of love.

As I sat and thought, my mind went back to the day that you and I first met, twenty-two years ago — twenty-two in February next. In twenty-two years more I could not forget that hideous first day in the city room of the *Morning Record.* I can see the great gloomy room, with its meagre gas-jets lighting up, here and there, a pale face at a desk, and bringing out in ghastly spots the ugliness of the ink-smeared walls. A winter rain was pouring down outside. I could feel its chill and damp in the room, though little of it was to be seen through the grimy window-panes. The composing-room in the rear sent a smell of ink and benzine to permeate the moist atmosphere. The rumble and shiver of the great presses printing the weekly came up from below. I sat there in my wet clothes and waited for my first assignment. I was eighteen, poor as a church mouse, green, desperately hopeful after a boy's fashion, and with nothing in my head but the Latin and Greek of my one single year at college. My spirit had sunk down far out of sight. My heart beat nervously at every sound of that awful city editor's voice, as he called up his soldiers one by one and assigned them to duty. I could only silently pray that he would " give me an easy one," and that I should not disgrace myself in the doing of it. By Jove, Will, what an old martinet Baldwin was, for all his good heart! Do you remember that sharp, crackling voice of his, and the awful " Be brief! be brief!" that always drove all capacity for condensation out of a man's head, and set him to stammering out his story with wordy incoherence? Baldwin is on the *Record* still. I wonder what poor devil is trembling at this hour under that disconcerting adjuration.

A wretched day that was! The hours went slow as grief. Smeary little bare-armed fiends trotted in from the composing-room and out again, bearing fluttering galley-proofs. Bedraggled, hollow-eyed men came in from the streets and set their soaked umbrellas to steam against the heater, and passed into the lion's den to feed him with news, and were sent out again to take up their half-cooked umbrellas and go forth to forage for more. Everyone, I thought, gave me one brief glance of contempt and curiosity, and put me out of his thoughts. Everyone had some business — everyone but me. The men who had been waiting with me were called up one by one and detailed to work. I was left alone.

Then a new horror came to torture my nervously active imagination. Had my superior officer forgotten his new recruit? Or could he find no task mean enough for my powers? This filled me at first with a sinking shame, and then with a hot rage and sense of wrong. Why should he thus slight me? Had I not a right to be tried, at least? Was there any duty he could find that I would not perform or die? I would go to him and tell him that I had come there to work; and would make him give me the work. No, I should simply be snubbed, and sent to my seat like a school-boy, or perhaps discharged on the spot. I must bear my humiliation in silence.

I looked up and saw you entering, with your bright, ruddy boy's face shining with wet, beaming a greeting to all the room. In my soul I cursed you, at a venture, for your lightheartedness and your look of cheery self-confidence. What a vast stretch of struggle and success set you above me — you, the reporter, above me, the novice! And just then came the awful summons — "Barclay! Barclay!"— I shall hear that strident note at the judgment day. I went in and got my orders, and came out with them, all in a sort of daze that must have made Baldwin think me an idiot. And then you came up to me and scraped acquaintance in a desultory way, to hide your kind intent; and gave me a hint or two as to how to obtain a full account of the biennial meeting of the Post-Pliocene Mineralogical Society, or whatever it was, without diving too deeply into the Post-Pliocene period. I would have fought for you to the death, at that moment.

'T was a small matter, but the friendship begun in manly and helpful kindness has gone on for twenty-two years in mutual faith and loyalty; and the growth dignifies the seed.

A sturdy growth it was in its sapling days. It was in the late spring that we decided to take the room together in St. Mark's Place. A big room and a poor room, indeed, on the third story of that "battered caravanserai," and for twelve long years it held us and our hopes and our despairs and our troubles and our joys.

I don't think I have forgotten one detail of that room. There is the generous old fireplace, insultingly bricked up by modern poverty, all save the meagre niche that holds our fire — when we can have a fire. There is the great second-hand table — our first purchase — where we sit and work for immortality in the scant intervals of working for life. Your drawer, with the manuscript of your "Concordance of Political Economy," is to the right. Mine is to the left; it holds the unfinished play, and the poems that might better have been unfinished. There are the two narrow cots — yours to the left of the door as you enter; mine to the right.

How strange that I can see it all so clearly, now that all is different!

Yet I can remember myself coming home at one o'clock at night, dragging my tired feet up those dark, still, tortuous stairs, gripping the shaky baluster for aid. I open the door — I can feel the little old-fashioned brass knob in my palm even now — and I look to the left. Ah, you are already at home and in bed.

I need not look toward the table. There is money — a little — in the common treasury; and, in accordance with our regular compact, I know there stand on that table twin bottles of beer, half a loaf of rye bread, and a double palm's-breadth of Swiss cheese. You are staying your hunger in sleep; for one may not eat until the other comes. I will wake you up, and we shall feast together and talk over the day that is dead and the day that is begun.

Strange, is it not, that I should have some trouble to realize that this is only a memory, — I, with my feet in the bearskin rug that it would have beggared the two of us, or a dozen like us, to purchase in those days. Strange that my mind should be wandering on the crude work of my boyhood and my early manhood. I who have won name and fame, as the world would say. I, to whom young men come for advice and encouragement, as to a tried veteran! Strange that I should be thinking of a time when even your true and tireless friendship could not quench a subtle hunger at my heart, a hunger for a more dear and intimate comradeship. I, with the tenderest of wives scarce out of my sight; even in her sleep she is no further from me than my own soul.

Strangest of all this, that the mad agony of grief, the passion of desolation that came upon me when our long partnership was dissolved for ever, should now be nothing but a memory, like other memories, to be summoned up out of the resting-places of the mind, toyed with, idly questioned, and dismissed with a sigh and a smile! What a real thing it was just ten years ago; what a very present pain! Believe me, Will, — yes, I want you to believe this — that in those first hours of loneliness I could have welcomed death; death would have fallen upon me as calmly as sleep has fallen upon my boy in the room beyond there.

You know nothing of this then; I suppose you but half believe it now; for our parting was manly enough. I kept as stiff an upper lip as you did, for all there was less hair on it. Perhaps it seems extravagant to you. But there was a deal of difference between our cases. You had turned your pen to money-making, at the call of love; you were going to Stillwater to marry the judge's daughter, and to become a great land-owner and mayor of Stillwater and millionaire — or what is it now? And much of this you foresaw or hoped for, at least. Hope is something. But for me? I was left in the third-story of a poor lodging-house in St. Mark's Place, my best friend gone from me; with neither remembrance nor hope of Love to live on, and with my last story back from *all* the magazines.

We will not talk about it. Let me get back to my pleasant library with the books and the pictures and the glancing fire-light, and me with my feet in your bearskin rug, listening to my wife's step in the next room.

To your ear, for our communion has been so long and so close that to either one of us the faintest inflection of the other's voice speaks clearer than formulated words; to your ear there must be something akin to a tone of regret — regret for the old days — in what I have just said. And would it be strange if there were? A poor soldier of fortune who had been set to a man's work before he had done with his meagre boyhood, who had passed from recruit to the place of a young veteran in that great, hard-fighting, unresting pioneer army of journalism; was he the man, all of a sudden, to stretch his toughened sinews out and let them relax in the glow of the home hearth? Would not his legs begin to twitch for the road; would he not be wild to feel again the rain in his weather-beaten face? Would you think it strange if at night he should toss in his white, soft bed, longing to change it for a blanket on the turf, with the broad procession of sunlit worlds sweeping over his head, beyond the blue spaces of the night? And even if the dear face on the pillow next him were to wake and look at him with reproachful surprise; and even if warm arms drew him back to his new allegiance; would not his heart in dreams go throbbing to the rhythm of the drum or the music of songs sung by the camp-fire?

It was so at the beginning, in the incredible happiness of the first year, and even after the boy's birth. Do you know, it was months before I could accept that boy as a *fact?* If, at any moment, he had vanished from my sight, crib and all, I should not have been surprised. I was not sure of him until he began to show his mother's eyes.

Yes, even in those days some of the old leaven worked in me. I had moments of that old barbaric freedom which we used to rejoice in — that feeling of being answerable to nothing in the world save my own will — the sense of untrammeled, careless power.

Do you remember the night that we walked till sunrise? You remember how hot it was at midnight, when we left the office, and how the moonlight on the statue above the City Hall seemed to invite us fieldward, where no gaslight glared, no torches flickered. So we walked idly northward, through the black, silence-stricken down-town streets; through that feverish, unresting central region that lies between the vileness of Houston Street and the calm and spacious dignity of the brown-stone ways, where the closed and darkened dwellings looked like huge tombs in the pallid light of the moon. We passed the suburban belt of shanties; we passed the garden-girt villas beyond them, and it was from the hill above Spuyten Duyvil that we saw the first color of the morning upon the face of the Palisades.

It would have taken very little in that moment to set us off to tramping the broad earth, for the pure joy of free wayfaring. What was there to hold us back? No tie of home or kin. All we had in the world to leave behind us was some futile scribbling on various sheets of paper. And of that sort of thing both our heads were full enough. I think it was but the veriest chance that, having begun that walk, we did not go on and get our fill of wandering, and ruin our lives.

Well, that same wild, adventurous spirit came upon me now and then. There were times when, for the moment, I forgot that I had a wife and a child. There were times when I remembered them as a burden. Why should I not say this? It is the history of every

married man, — at least of every manly man, — though
he be married to the best woman in the world. It means
no lack of love. It is as unavoidable as the leap of the
blood in you that answers a trumpet-call.

At first I was frightened, and fought against it as
against something that might grow upon me. I re-
proached myself for disloyalty in thought. Ah! what
need had *I* to fight? What need had I to choke down
rebellious fancies, while my wife's love was working
that miracle that makes two spirits one.

What is it, this union that comes to us as a surprise,
and remains for all outside an incommunicable mystery?
What is this that makes our unmarried love seem so
slight and childish a thing? You and I, who know it,
know that it is no mere fruit of intimacy and usage,
although in its growth it keeps pace with these. We
know that in some subtle way it has been given to a
man to see a woman's soul as he sees his own, and to a
woman to look into a man's heart as if it were, indeed,
hers. But the friend who sits at my table, seeing that
my wife and I understand each other at a simple meeting of the eyes, make no more of it than he does of the
glance of intelligence which, with close friends, often
takes the place of speech. He never dreams of the
sweet delight with which we commune together in a
language that he cannot understand — that he cannot
hear — a language that has no formulated words, feeling answering feeling.

It is not wonderful that I should wish to give expression to the gratitude with which I have seen my

life made to blossom thus; my thankfulness for the love which has made me not only a happier, but, I humbly believe, a wiser and a better-minded man. But I know too well the hopelessness of trying to find words to describe what, were I a poet, my best song might but faintly, faintly echo.

I thought I heard a rustle behind me just now. In a little while my wife will come softly into the room, and softly up to where I am sitting, stepping silently across your bearskin rug, and will lay one hand softly on my left shoulder, while the other slips down this arm with which I write, until it falls and closes lightly, yet with loving firmness, on my hand that holds the pen. And I shall say, "Only the last words to Will and his wife, dear." And she will release my hand, and will lift her own, I think, to caress the patch of gray hair on my temple; it is a way she has, as though it were some pitiful scar, and she will say, "Give them my love, and tell them they must not fail us this Christmas. I want them to see how our Willy has grown." And when she says "Our Willy," the hand on my shoulder will instinctively close a little, clingingly; and she will bend her head, and put her face close to mine, and I shall turn to look into her eyes.

*   *   *   *   *   *

Bear with me, my dear Will, until I have told you why I have written this letter and what it means. I have concealed one thing from you for the last six months. I have disease of the heart, and the doctor has told me that I may die at any moment. Somehow,

I think — I know the moment is close at hand; I shall soon go to that narrow cot on the right of the door, and I do not believe I shall wake up in the morning with the sun in my eyes, to look across the room and see that its companion is gone.

For I am in the old room, Will, as you know, and it is not ten years since you went away, but two days. The picture that has seemed real to me as I wrote these pages is fading, and the thin gas-jet flickers and sinks as it always did in these first morning hours. I can hear the roar of the last Harlem train swell and sink, and the sharp clink of car-bells break the silence that follows. The wind is gasping and struggling in the chimney, and blowing a white powdery ash down on the hearth. I have just burnt my poems and the play. Both the table drawers are empty now; and soon enough the two empty chairs will stare at each other across the bare table. What a wild dream have I dreamt in all this emptiness! Just now, I thought indeed that it was true. I thought I heard a woman's step behind me, and I turned —

Peace be with you, Will, in the fullness of your love. I am going to sleep. Perhaps I shall dream it all again, and shall hear that soft footfall when the turn of the night comes, and the pale light through the ragged blind, and the end of a long loneliness.

After I am dead, I wish you to think of me not as I was, but as I wanted to be. I have tried to show you that I have led by your side a happier and dearer life of hope and aspiration than the one you saw. I have

tried to leave your memory a picture of me that you will
not shrink from calling up when you have a quiet hour
and time for thought of the friend whom you knew
well; but whom you may, perhaps, know better now
that he is dead.

REGINALD BARCLAY.

*   *   *   *   *   *

II.

THE PARAGRAPH.

[From the *New York Herald* of Nov. 18, 1883.]

Reginald Barclay, a journalist, was found dead in his
bed at 15 St. Mark's Place, yesterday morning. No
inquest was held, as Mr. Barclay had been known to be
suffering from disease of the heart, and his death was
not unexpected. The deceased came originally from
Oneida County, and was regarded as a young journalist of considerable promise. He had been for some
years on the city staff of the *Record*, and was the
correspondent of several out-of-town papers. He had
also contributed to the monthly magazines, occasional
poems and short stories, which showed the possession,
in some measure, of the imaginative faculty. Mr. Barclay was about thirty years of age, and unmarried.

PLAYING A PART:

A COMEDY FOR AMATEUR ACTING.

BY BRANDER MATTHEWS.

The Scene is a handsomely-furnished parlor, with a general air of home comfort. A curtained window on each side of the central fireplace would light the room if it were not evening, as the lamp on the work-table in the centre of the room informs us. At one side of the work-table is the wife, winding a ball of worsted from a skein which her husband holds in his hands.

HE (*looking at watch, aside*). This wool takes as long to wind up as a bankrupt estate. (*Fidgets.*)

She. Do keep still, Jack! Stop fidgeting and jumping around.

He. When you pull the string, Jenny, I am always a jumping-jack to dance attendance on you.

She (*seriously*). Very pretty, indeed! It was true too — once — before we were married : now you lead me a different dance.

He. I am your partner still.

She (*sadly*). But the figure is always the Ladies' Chain.

He (*aside*). If I don't get away soon I sha'n't be able to do any work to-night. — (*Aloud*). What do you mean by that solemn tone?

She. Oh, nothing — nothing of any consequence.

179

He (aside). We look like two fools acting in private theatricals.

She (finishing ball of worsted). That will do: thank you. Do not let me detain you: I know you are in a hurry.

He. I have my work to do.

She. So it seems; and it takes all day and half the night.

He (rising and going to fireplace). I am working hard for our future happiness.

She (quietly). I should like a little of the happiness now.

He (standing with back to fireplace). Are you unhappy?

She. Oh no — not very.

He. Do you not have everything you wish?

She. Oh yes — except the one thing I want most.

He. Well, my dear, I am at home as much as I can be.

She. So you think I meant you?

He (embarrassed). Well — I did suppose — that —

She. Yes, I used to want you. The days were long enough while you were away, and I waited for your return. Now I have been alone so much that I am getting accustomed to solitude. And I do not really know what it is I do want. I am listless, nervous, good-for-nothing —

He (gallantly). You are good enough for me.

She. You did think so once; and perhaps you would think so again — if you could spare the time to get acquainted with me.

He (*surprised*). Jenny, are you ill?

She. Not more so than usual. I was bright enough two years ago, when we were married. But for two years I have not lived, I have vegetated; more like a plant than a human being; and even plants require some sunshine.

He (*aside*). I have never heard her talk like this before. I don't understand it. — (*Aloud.*) Why, Jenny, you speak as if I were a cloud over your life.

She. Do I? Well, it does not matter.

He. I try to be a good husband, don't I?

She (*indifferently*). As well as you know how, I suppose.

He. Do I deprive you of anything you want?

She (*impatiently*). Of course you do not.

He. I work hard, I know, but when I go out in the evening now and then —

She (*aside*). Six nights every week. (*Sighing.*)

He. I really work. There are husbands who say they are at work when they are at the club playing poker: now I am really working.

She (*impatiently*). You have no small vices. (*Rising.*) Is there no work calling you away to-night? Why are you not off?

He (*looking at watch*). I am a little late, that's a fact: still, I can do what I have to do if I work like a horse.

She. Have you to draw a conveyance? That is the old joke.

He. This is no joke. It's a divorce suit.

She (*quickly*). Is it that Lightfoot person again?

He. It is Mrs. Lightfoot's case. She is a very fine woman, and her husband has treated her shamefully.

She. Better than the creature deserved, I dare say. You will win her case for her?

He. I shall do my best.

She (*sarcastically*). No doubt. — (*Aside.*) I hate that woman! (*Crosses the room and sits on sofa on the right of the fireplace.*)

He. But the result of a lawsuit is generally a toss-up; and heads do not always win.

She. I wish you luck this time — for her husband's sake: he'll be glad to be rid of her. But I doubt it: you can't get up any sympathy by exhibiting her to the jury: she isn't good-looking enough.

He (*quickly*). She's a very fine woman indeed.

She (*aside*). How eagerly he defends her! — (*Aloud.*) She's a great big, tall, giantess creature, with a face like a wax doll and a head of hair like a Circassian Girl. No juryman will fall in love with her.

He. How often have I told you that Justice does not consider persons! Now, in the eye of the law —

She (*interrupting*). Do you acknowledge that the law has but one eye and can see only one side?

He. Are you jealous? (*Crossing and standing in front of her.*)

She. Jealous of this Mrs. Lightfoot? (*Laughs.*) Ridiculous!

He. I am glad of it, for I think a jealous woman has a very poor opinion of herself.

She (forcibly). And it is her business which takes you out to-night?

He (going toward the left-hand door). I have to go across to the Bar Association to look up some points, and —

She (rising quickly). And you can just send me a cab. I shall go to Mrs. Playfair's to rehearse again for the private theatricals.

He (annoyed, coming back). But I had asked you to give it up.

She (with growing excitement). And I had almost determined to give it up, but I have changed my mind. That's a woman's privilege, isn't it? I am tired of spending my evenings by myself. ·

He. Now be reasonable, Jenny: I must work.

She. And I must play — in the private theatricals.

He. But I don't like private theatricals.

She. Don't you? I do.

He. And I particularly dislike amateur actors.

She. Do you? I don't. I like some of them very much; and some of them like me, too.

He. The deuce they do!

She. Tom Thursby and Dick Carey and Harry Wylde were all disputing who should make love to me.

He. Make love to you?

She. In the play — in *Husbands and Wives.*

He. Do you mean to say that you are going to act on the stage with those brainless idiots?

She (interrupting). Do not call my friends names: it is in bad taste.

He. What will people say when they see my wife pawed and clawed by those fellows?

She. Let them say what they please. Do you think I care for the tittle-tattle of the riffraff of society?

He. But, Jenny — (*Brusquely.*) Confound it! I have no patience with you!

She. So I have discovered. But you need not lose your temper here, and swear. Go outside and do it, and leave me alone, as I am every evening.

He. You talk as if I ill-treated you.

She (sarcastically.) Do I? That is very wicked of me, isn't it? You take the best possible care of me, you are ever thinking of me, and you never leave my side for a moment. Oh no, you do not ill-treat me — or abuse me — or neglect me (*breaking down*) — or make me miserable. There is nothing the matter with me, of course. But you never will believe I have a heart until you have broken it! (*Sinking on chair, C.*)

He (crossing to her). You are excited, I see; still, I must say this is a little too much.

She (starting up). Don't come near me! (*Sarcastically.*) Don't let me keep you from your work (*going to door R. 2d E*), and don't fail to send me a cab. At last I revolt against your neglect.

He (indignantly protesting). My neglect? Do you mean to say I neglect you? My conscience does not reproach me.

She (at the door on the right). That's because you haven't any! (*Exit, slamming door*).

He (alone). I never saw her go on that way before. What can be the matter with her? She is not like

herself at all : she is low-spirited and nervous. Now,
I never could see why women had any nerves. I wonder if she really thinks that I neglect her? I should
be sorry, very sorry, if she did. I 'll not go out to-night :
I 'll stay at home and have a quiet evening at my own
fireside. (*Sits in chair in the centre*). I think that
will bring her round. I 'd like to know what has made
her act like this. Has she been reading any sentimental
trash, I wonder? (*Sees book in work-basket.*) Now,
here 's some yellow-covered literature. (*Takes it up.*)
Why, it 's that confounded play, *Husbands and Wives.*
Let me see the silly stuff. (*Reads :*) " My darling, one
more embrace, one last, long, loving kiss ; " and then
he hugs her and kisses her. (*Rising.*) And she
thinks I 'll have her play a part like that? How should
I look while that was going on? Can 't she find something else? (*At work-table.*) Here is another. (*Takes
up second pamphlet.*) No, it is a *Guide to the Passions.* I fear I need no guide to get into a passion. I
doubt if there 's as much hugging and kissing in this as
in the other one. (*Reads :*) " It is impossible to describe all the effects of the various passions, but a few
hints are here given as to how the more important may
be delineated." (*Spoken.*) This is interesting. If
ever I have to delineate a passion I shall fall back on
this guide. (*Reads :*) " Love is a —" (*Reads hastily
and unintelligibly :*) " When successful, love author-
izes the fervent embrace of the beloved ! " The deuce
it does! And I find my wife getting instruction from
this Devil's text-book ! A little more and I should be
jealous. (*Looks at book.*) Ah, here is jealousy : now

let's see how I ought to feel. (*Reads:*) "Jealousy is a mixture of passions and —" (*Reads hastily and unintelligibly.*) Not so bad! I believe I could act up to these instructions. (*Jumping up.*) And I will! My wife wants acting: she shall have it! She complains of monotony: she shall have variety! "Jealousy is a mixture of passions." I'll be jealous: I'll give her a mixture of passions. I'll take a leaf out of her book, and I'll find a cure for these nerves of her's. I'll learn my part at once: we'll have some private theatricals to order. (*Walks up and down, studying book.*)

She re-enters, with bonnet on and cloak over her arm, and stands in surprise, watching him.

She. You here still?

He. Yes.

She. Have you ordered a cab for me?

He. No.

She. And why not?

He (*aside*). Now's my chance. Mixture of passions — I'll try suspicion first. — (*Aloud.*) Because I do not approve of the people you are going to meet — these Thursbys and Careys and Wyldes.

She (*calmly sitting on sofa*). Perhaps you would like to revise my visiting-list, and tell the servant whom I am to receive.

He. You may see what ladies you please —

She (*interrupting*). Thank you; still, I do not please to see Mrs. Lightfoot.

He (*annoyed*). I say nothing of her.

She. Oh dear, no! I dare say you keep it as secret as you can.

He (*aside*). Simple suspicion is useless. What's next? (*Glances in pamphlet :*) "Peevish personalities." I will pass on to peevish personalities. — (*Aloud.*) Now, these men, these fellows who strut about the stage for an idle hour, who are they? This Tom Thursby, who wanted to make love to you — who is he?

She. Are you going to ask many questions? Is this catechism a long one? If it is, I may as well lay aside my shawl.

He. Who is he, I say, I insist upon knowing.

She. He's a good enough fellow in his way.

He (*sternly*). He had best beware how he gets in *my* way.

She (*aside*). There's a great change in his manner: I do not understand it.

He. And this Dick Carey — who is he? (*Stalking toward her.*)

She (*starting up and crossing*). Are you trying to frighten me by this violence?

He (*aside*). It is producing an effect.

She. But I am not afraid of you, if I am a weak woman and you are a strong man.

He (*aside*). It is going all right. — (*Aloud, fiercely.*) Answer me at once! Is this Carey married?

She. I believe he is.

He. You believe! Don't you know? Does his wife act with these strollers? Have you not seen her ?

She. I have never seen her. She and her husband
are like the two buckets in a well: they never turn up
together. They meet only to clash, and one is always
throwing cold water on the other.

He. And Harry Wylde! Is he married?

She. Yes; and his wife is always keeping him in
hot water.

He. And so he comes to you for consolation?

She (laughing). He needs no consoling: he has
always such a flow of spirits.

He. I've heard the fellow drank.

She (surprised, aside). Can Jack be jealous? I
wish I could think so, for then I might hope he still
loved me.

He. And do you suppose I can allow you to associate with these fellows, who all want to make love
to you?

She (aside, joyfully). He *is* jealous! The dear
boy!

He (fiercely). Do you think I can permit this,
madam?

She (aside). "Madam!" I could hug him for loving me enough to call me "madam" like that. But I
must not give in too soon.

He. Have you nothing to say for yourself? Can
you find no words to defend yourself, woman?

She (aside). "Woman!" He calls me "woman!"
I can forgive him anything now.

He. Are you dumb, woman? Have you naught to
say?

She (gleefully, aside). I had no idea I had married

an Othello! (*She sees the pillow on the sofa, and, crossing to it quietly, hides the pillow behind the sofa.*)

He (*aside*). What did she mean by that? — (*Aloud, fiercely.*) Do you intend to deny —

She (*interrupting*). I have nothing to deny, I have nothing to conceal.

He. Do you deny that you confessed these fellows sought to make love to you?

She. I do not deny that. (*Mischievously.*) But I never thought you would worry about such trifles.

He. Trifles! madam? Trifles, indeed! (*Glances in book, and quoting:*)

> "Trifles light as air
> Are to the jealous confirmations strong
> As proofs of holy writ."

She (*surprised aside*). Where did he get his blank verse?

He (*aside*). That seemed to tell. I'll give her some more. (*Glancing in pamphlet, and quoting:*)

> "But, alas, to make me
> A fixed figure for the time of scorn
> To point his slow, unmoving finger at!"

She (*aside, jumping up with indignation*). Why, it *is Othello* he is quoting! He is acting! He is positively playing a part! It is shameful of him! It's not real jealousy: it's a sham. Oh, the wretch! But I'll pay him back! I'll make him jealous without any make-believe.

He (*aside*). I'm getting on capitally. I'm making a strong impression: I am rousing her out of her nervousness. I doubt if she will want any more private theatricals now. I don't think I shall have to repeat the lesson. This *Guide to the Passions* is a first-rate book: I'll keep one in the house all the time.

She (aside). If he plays Othello, I can play Iago. I'll give his jealousy something to feed on. I have no blank verse for him, but I'll make him blank enough before I am done with him. Oh, the villain!

He (aside). Now let me try threatening. (*Glancing in book:*) "Pity the sorrows of a poor old man" —I've got the wrong place. That's not threatening —that's senility. (*Turning over page.*) Ah, here it is.

She (aside). And he thinks he can jest with a woman's heart and not be punished? Oh, the wickedness of man!—(*Forcibly*). Oh, if mamma were only here, now!

He (threateningly). Who are these fellows? This Tom, Dick and Harry are — are they — (*hesitates, and glances in pamphlet*) are they "framed to make women false?"

She (aside). Why, he's got a book! It's my ·*Guide to the Passions.* The wretch has actually been copying his jealousy out of my own book. (*Aloud, with pretended emotion*). Dear me, Jack, you never before objected to my little flirtations. (*Aside, watching him*). How will he like that?

He (aside, puzzled). "Little flirtations!" I don't like that—I don't like it at all.

She. They have all been attentive, of course—

He (aside). "Of course!" I don't like that, either.

She. But I did not think you would so take to heart a few innocent endearments.

He (starting). "Innocent endearments!" Do you mean to say that they offer you any "innocent endearments?"

She (quietly). Don't be so boisterous, Jack: you will crush my book.

He (looking at pamphlet crushed in his hand, and throwing it from him, aside). Confound the book! I do not need any prompting now. — *(Aloud.)* Which of these men has dared to offer you any "innocent endearments?"

She (hesitatingly). Well — I don't know — that I ought to tell you — since you take things so queerly. But Tom —

He (forcibly). Tom?

She. Mr. Thursby, I mean. He and I are very old friends, you know — I believe we are third cousins or so — and of course I don't stand on ceremony with him.

He. And he does not stand on ceremony with you, I suppose?

She. Oh, no. In fact, we are first-rate friends. Indeed, when Dick Carey wanted to make love to me, he was quite jealous.

He. Oh, *he* was jealous, was he? The fellow's impudence is amazing! When I meet him I'll give him a piece of my mind.

She (demurely). Are you sure you can spare it!

He. Don't irritate me too far, Jenny: I've a temper of my own.

She. You seem to have lost it now.

He. Do you not see that I am in a heat about this thing? How can you sit there so calmly? You keep cool like a — (*hesitates*) like a —

She (*interrupting*). Like a burning-glass, I keep cool myself while setting you on fire? Exactly so, and I suppose you would prefer me to be a looking-glass in which you could see only yourself?

He. A wife should reflect her husband's image, and not that of a pack of fools.

She. Come, come, Jack, you are not jealous?

He. "Jealous!" Of course I am not jealous, but I am very much annoyed.

She. I am glad that you are not jealous, for I have always heard that a jealous man has a very poor opinion of himself. — (*Aside.*) There's one for him.

He. I am not jealous, but I will probe this thing to the bottom; I must know the truth.

She (*aside*). He *is* jealous now; and this is real: I am sure it is.

He. Go on, tell me more : I must get at the bottom facts. There's nothing like truth.

She (*aside*). There is nothing like it in what he's learning.

He (*aside*). This Carey is harmless enough, and he can't help talking. He's a — he's a telescope; you have only to draw him out, and anybody can see through him. I'll get hold of him, draw him out, and then shut him up! (*Crossing excitedly.*)

She (*aside*). How much more his real jealousy moves me than his pretence of it! He seems very much affected : no man could be as jealous as he is unless he was very much in love.

He (*with affected coolness*). You have told me about Tom and Dick; pray, have you nothing to say about Harry ?

She. Mr. Wylde? (*Enthusiastically.*) He is a man after my own heart !

He. So he is after it ? (*Savagely.*) Just let me get after him !

She (*coolly*). Well, if you do not like his attentions, you can take him apart and tell him so.

He (*vindictively*). If I took him apart he'd never get put together again !

She. Mr. Wylde is very much afraid of his wife, but when she is not there he is more devoted than either of the others.

He. "More devoted !" What else shall I hear, I wonder ?

She. It was he who had to kiss me.

He (*startled*). What ?

She. I told him not to do it. I knew I should blush if he kissed me : I always do.

He (*in great agitation*). You always do ? Has this man ever — (*Breaking down.*) Oh, Jenny ! Jenny ! you do not know what you are doing. I do not blame you — it is not your fault : it is mine. I did not know how much I loved you, and I find it out now, when it is perhaps too late.

She (*aside*). How I have longed for a few words of love like these ! and they have come at last !

He. I have been too selfish ; I have thought too

much of my work and too little of your happiness. I see now what a mistake I have made.

She (*aside*). I cannot sit still here and see him waste his love in the air like this.

He. I shall turn over a new leaf. If you will let me I shall devote myself to you, taking care of you and making you happy.

She (*aside*). If he had only spoken like that before!

He. I will try to win you away from these associates: I am sure that in your heart you do not care for them. (*Crossing to her.*) You know that I love you: can I not hope to win you back to me?

She (*aside*). Once before he spoke to me of his love: I can remember every tone of his voice, every word he said.

He. Jenny, is my task hopeless?

She (*quietly crossing to arm-chair*). The task is easy, Jack. (*Smiling.*) Perhaps you think too much of these associates: perhaps you think a good deal more of them than I do. In fact, I am sure that to-night you were the one who took to private theatricals first. By the way, where's my *Guide to the Passions?* Have you seen it lately?

He (*half comprehending*). Your *Guide to the Passions?* A book with a yellow cover? I think I *have* seen it.

She. I saw it last in your hand — just after you had been quoting *Othello.*

He. *Othello?* Oh, then you know —

She (*smiling*). Yes, I know. I saw, I understood, and I retaliated on the spot.

He. You retaliated?

She. I paid you off in your own coin — counterfeit, like yours.

He (joyfully). Then Tom did not make love to you?

She. Oh, yes he did — in the play.

He. And Dick is not devoted?

She. Yes, he is — in the play.

He. And Harry did not try to kiss you?

She. Indeed he did — in the play.

He. Then you have been playing a part?

She. Have n't you?

He. Have n't I? Certainly not. At least — Well, at least I will say nothing more about Tom or Dick or Harry.

She. And I will say nothing more of Mrs. Lightfoot.

He (dropping in chair to her right). Mrs. Lightfoot is a fine woman, my dear (*she looks up*), but she is not my style at all. Besides, you know, it was only as a matter of business, for the sake of our future prospects, that I took her part.

She (throwing him skein of wool). And it is only for the sake of our future happiness that I have been playing mine.

He holds the wool and she winds the ball, and the curtain falls, leaving them in the same position its rising discovered them in.

LOVE IN OLD CLOATHES.

NEWE YORK, yᵉ 1ˢᵗ Aprile, 1883.

Yᵉ worste of my ailment is this, yᵗ it groweth not
Less with much nursinge, but is like to those fevres
wᶜʰ yᵉ leeches Starve, 'tis saide, for that yᵉ more Bloode
there be in yᵉ Sicke man's Bodie, yᵉ more foode is there
for yᵉ Distemper to feede upon. — And it is moste fit-
tinge yᵗ I come backe to yᵉ my Journall (wherein I
have not writt a Lyne these manye months) on yᵉ 1ˢᵗ of
Aprile, beinge in some Sort myne owne foole and yᵉ
foole of Love, and a poore Butt on whome his hearte
hath play'd a Sorry tricke. —

For it is surelie a strange happenninge, that I, who
am ofte accompted a man of yᵉ Worlde, (as yᵉ Phrase
goes,) sholde be soe Overtaken and caste downe lyke
a Schoole-boy or a countrie Bumpkin, by a meere
Mayde, & sholde set to Groaninge and Sighinge, &, for
that She will not have me Sighe to Her, to Groaninge
and Sighinge on paper, wᶜʰ is yᵉ greter Foolishnesse in
Me, yᵗ some one maye read it Here-after, who hath
taken his dose of yᵉ same Physicke, and made no Wrye
faces over it; in wᶜʰ case I doubte I shall be much
laugh'd at. — Yet soe much am I a foole, and soe enam-
our'd of my Foolishnesse, yᵗ I have a sorte of Shame-
full Joye in tellinge, even to my Journall, yᵗ I am

196

mightie deepe in Love withe y^e yonge Daughter of Mistresse Ffrench, and all maye knowe what an Angell is y^e Daughter, since I have chose Mrs French for my Mother in Lawe. — (Though she will have none of my choosinge.) — and I likewise take comforte in y^e Fancie, y^t this poore Sheete, wh^{on} I write, may be made of $\ddot{y}^e$ Raggs of some lucklesse Lover, and maye y^e more readilie drinke up my complaininge Inke. —

This muche I have learnt y^t Fraunce distilles not, nor y^e Indies growe not, y^e Remedie for my Aile. — For when I 1st became sensible of y^e folly of my Suite, I tooke to drynkinge & smoakinge, thinkinge to cure my minde, but all I got was a head ache, for fellowe to my Hearte ache. — A sorrie Payre! — I then made Shifte, for a while, withe a Bicycle, but breakinge of Bones mendes no breakinge of Heartes, and 60 myles a Daye bringes me no nearer to a Weddinge. — This being Lowe Sondaye, (wch my Hearte telleth me better than ye Allmanack,) I will goe to Churche ; wh. I maye chaunce to see her. — Laste weeke, her Eastre bonnett vastlie pleas'd me, beinge most cunninglie devys'd in ye mode of oure Grandmothers, and verie lyke to a coales Scuttle, of white satine. —

2nd Aprile.

I trust I make no more moane, than is just for a man in my case, but there is small comforte in lookinge at ye backe of a white Satine bonnett for two Houres, and I maye saye as much. — Neither any cheere in Her goinge out of ye Churche, & Walkinge downe ye Avenue, with a Puppe by ye name of Williamson.

Because a man have a Hatt with a Brimme to it like ye Poope-Decke of a Steam-Shippe, and breeches lyke ye Case of an umbrella, and have loste money on Hindoo, he is not therefore in ye beste Societie.— I made this observation, at ye Clubbe, last nighte, in ye hearinge of W^{mson}, who made a mightie Pretence to reade ye Sp^t of ye Tymes.— I doubte it was scurvie of me, but it did me muche goode.

7th Aprile.

Y^e manner of my meetinge with Her and fallinge in Love with Her (for ye two were of one date) is thus. —I was made acquainte withe Her on a Wednesdaie, at ye House of Mistresse Varick, ('twas a Reception,) but did not hear Her Name, nor She myne, by reason of ye noise, and of M^{rsse} Varick having but lately a newe sett of Teethe, of wh. she had not yet gott, as it were, ye just Pitche and accordance. — I sayde to Her that ye Weather was warm for that season of ye yeare. — She made answer She thought I was right, for Mr Williamson had saide ye same thinge to Her not a minute past. — I tolde Her She muste not holde it originall or an Invention of W^{mson}, for ye Speache had beene manie yeares in my Familie. — Answer was made, She wolde be muche bounden to me if I wolde maintaine ye Rightes of my Familie, and lett all others from usinge of my propertie, when perceivinge Her to be of a livelie Witt, I went about to ingage her in converse, if onlie so I mightie looke into Her Eyes, wh. were of a coloure suche as I have never seene

before, more like to a Pansie, or some such flower,
than anything else I can compair with them.—Short-
lie we grew most friendlie, so that She did aske me if
I colde keepe a Secrett.—I answering I colde, She
saide She was anhungered, having Shopp'd all y⁰ fore-
noone since Breakfast.—She pray'd me to gett Her
some Foode.—What, I ask'd.—She answer'd merrilie,
a Beafesteake.—I tolde Her yᵗ that *Confection* was
not on yᵉ Side-Boarde; but I presentlie brought Her
such as there was, & She beinge behinde a Screane, I
stoode in yᵉ waie, so yᵗ none mighte see Her, & She
did eate and drynke as followeth, to witt—

iij cupps of Bouillon (wᶜʰ is a Tea, or Tisane, of
  Beafe, made verie hott & thinne)
iv Alberte biscuit
ij éclairs
 i creame-cake

together with divers small cates and comfeits whᵒᶠ I
know not yᵉ names.

So yᵗ I was grievously afeared for Her Digestion,
leste it be over-tax'd. Saide this to Her, however
addinge it was my Conceite, yᵗ by some Processe, lyke
Alchemie, whᵇʸ yᵉ baser metals are transmuted into
golde, so yᵉ grosse mortall foode was on Her lippes
chang'd to yᵉ fabled Nectar & Ambrosia of yᵉ Gods.—
She tolde me 't was a sillie Speache, yet seam'd not
ill-pleas'd withall.—She hath a verie prettie Fashion,
or Tricke, of smilinge, when She hath made an end of
speakinge, and layinge Her finger upon Her nether

Lippe, like as She wolde bid it be stille. — After some more Talke, whⁱⁿ She show'd that Her Witt was more deepe, and Her minde more seriouslie inclin'd, than I had Thoughte from our first Jestinge, She beinge call'd to go thence, I did see Her mother, whose face I knewe, & was made sensible, y^t I had given my Hearte to ye daughter of a House wh. with myne owne had longe been at grievous Feud, for ye folly of oure Auncestres. — Havinge come to wh. heavie momente in my Tale, I have no Patience to write more to-nighte.

22nd Aprile.

I was mynded to write no more in ye journall, for veric Shame's sake, y^t I shoude so complayne, lyke a Childe, whose toic is taken f^m him, butt (mayhapp for it is nowe ye fulle Moone, & a moste greavous period for them y^t are Love-strucke) I am fayne, lyke ye Drunkarde who maye not abstayne f^m his cupp, to sett me anewe to recordinge of My Dolorous mishapp. — When I sawe Her agayn, She beinge aware of my name, & of ye division betwixt oure Houses, wolde have none of me, butt I wolde not be putt Off, & made bolde to question Her, why She sholde showe me suche exceed^g Coldness. — She answer'd 't was wel knowne what Wronge my Grandefather had done Her G.father. — I saide, She confounded me with My G.father — we were nott ye same Persone, he beinge muche my Elder, & besydes Dead. — She w^d have it, 't was no matter for jestinge. — I tolde Her I wolde be resolv'd, what grete Wronge y^{is} was. — Y^e more for to make Speache thⁿ for mine owne advertisem^t, for I

knewe wel ye whole Knaverie, wh. She rehears'd, Howe
my G.father had cheated Her G.father of Landes upp
ye River, with more, howe my G.father had impounded
ye Cattle of Hern. — I made answer, 't was foolishnesse,
in my mynde, for ye iii^d Generation to so quarrell over
a Parsel of rascallie Landes, y^t had long ago beene
solde for Taxes, y^t as to ye Cowes, I wolde make them
goode, & th^r Produce & Offspringe, if it tooke ye whole
Wash^tn Markett. — She however tolde me y^t ye Ffrenche
family had ye where w^al to buye what they lack'd in
Butter, Beafe & Milke, and likewise in *Veale*, wh.
laste I tooke muche to Hearte, wh. She seeinge, became
more gracious &, on my pleadinge, accorded y^t I sholde
have ye Privilege to speake with Her when we next
met. — Butt neyther then, nor at any other Tyme
th^after wolde She suffer me to visitt Her. So I was
harde putt to it to compass waies of gettinge to see
Her at such Houses as She mighte be att, for Routs or
Feasts, or ye lyke. —

But though I sawe Her manie tymes, oure converse
was ever of y^is Complex^n, & ye accursed G.father satt
downe, and rose upp with us. — Yet colde I see by
Her aspecte, y^t I had in some sorte Her favoure, & y^t
I mislyk'd Her not so gretelie as She w^d have me
thinke. — So y^t one daie, ('t was in Januarie, & verie
colde,) I, beinge moste distrackt, saide to Her, I had
tho't 'twolde pleasure Her more, to be friends w. a man,
who had a knave for a G.father, y^n with One who had
no G.father att alle, lyke W^mson (ye Puppe). — She
made answer, I was exceedinge fresshe, or some such
matter. She cloath'd her thoughte in phrase more

befittinge a Gentlewoman. — Att this I colde no longer contayne myself, but tolde Her roundlie, I lov'd Her, & 't was my Love made me soe unmannerlie. — And w. y^ls speache I att ye leaste made an End of my Uncertantie, for She bade me speake w. Her no more. — I wolde be determin'd, whether I was Naught to Her. — She made Answer She colde not justlie say I was Naught, seeing y^t wh^ever She mighte bee, I was One too manie. — I saide, 't was some Comforte, I had even a Place in Her thoughtes, were it onlie in Her disfavour. — She saide, my Solace was indeede grete, if it kept pace with ye measure of Her Disfavour, for, in plain Terms, She hated me, & on her intreatinge of me to goe, I went. — Y^ls happ'd att ye house of M^res Varicke, wh. I 1st met Her, who (M^res Varicke) was for staying me, y^t I might eate some Ic'd Cream, butt of a Truth I was chill'd to my Taste allreadie. — Albeit I afterwards tooke to walkinge of ye Streets till near Midnight. — 'Twas as I saide before in Januarie & exceedinge colde.

20th Maie.

How wearie is y^ls dulle procession of ye Yeare! For it irketh my Soule y^t each Monthe shoude come so aptlie after ye Month afore, & Nature looke so Smug, as She had done some grete thinge. — Surelie if she make no Change, she hath work'd no Miracle, for we knowe wel, what we maye look for. — Y^e Vine under my Window hath broughte forth Purple Blossoms, as itt hath eache Springe these xii Yeares. — I wolde have had them Redd, or Blue, or I knowe not what Coloure, for I am sicke of likinge of Purple a Dozen Springes in

Order. — And wh. moste galls me is y^is, I knowe howe y^is sadd Rounde will goe on, & Maie give Place to June, & she to July, & onlie my Hearte blossom not nor my Love growe no greener.

2nd June.

I and my Foolishnesse, we laye Awake last night till ye Sunrise gun, wh. was Shott att 4½ o'ck, & wh. beinge hearde in y^t stillnesse fm. an Incredible Distance, seem'd lyke as 't were a Full Stopp, or Period putt to y^is Wakinge-Dreminge, wh^at I did turne a newe Leafe in my Counsells, and after much Meditation, have commenc't a newe Chapter, wh. I hope maye leade to a better Conclusion, than them y^t came afore. — For I am nowe resolv'd, & havinge begunn wil carry to an Ende, y^t if I maie not over-come my Passion, I maye at ye least over-com ye Melanchollie, & Spleene, borne y^of, & beinge a Lover, be none ye lesse a Man. — To wh. Ende I have come to y^is Resolution, to depart fm. ye Towne, & to goe to ye Countrie-House of my Frend, Will Winthrop, who has often intreated me, & has instantly urg'd, y^t I sholde make him a Visitt. — And I take much Shame to myselfe, y^t I have not given him y^is Satisfaction since he was married, wh. is nowe ii Yeares. — A goode Fellowe, & I minde me a grete Burden to his Frends when he was in Love, in wh. Plight I mockt him, who am nowe, I much feare me, mockt myselfe.

3rd June.

Pack'd my cloathes, beinge Sundaye. Y^e better ye Daie, ye better ye Deede.

4th June.

Goe downe to Babylon to-daye.

5th June.

Att Babylon, att yᵉ Cottage of Will Winthrop, wh. is no Cottage, but a grete House, Red, w. Verandahs, & builded in yᵉ Fashⁿ of Her Maiestie Q. Anne. — Found a mighty Housefull of People. — Will, his Wife, a verie proper fayre Ladie, who gave me moste gracious Reception, Mʳˢ Smithe, yᵉ ii Gresham girles (knowne as yᵉ Titteringe Twins), Bob White, Virginia Kinge & her Mothʳ, Clarence Winthrop, & yᵉ whole Alexander Family. — A grete Gatheringe for so earlie in yᵉ Summer. — In yᵉ Afternoone play'd Lawne-Tenniss. — Had for Partner one of yᵉ Twinns, agˢᵗ Clarence Winthrop & yᵉ other Twinn, wh. by beinge Confus'd, I loste iii games. — Was voted a Duffer. — Clarence Winthrop moste unmannerlie merrie. — He call'd me yᵉ Sad-Ey'd Romeo, & lykewise cut down yᵉ Hammocke whⁱⁿ I laye, allso tied up my Cloathes wh. we were att Bath. — He sayde, he Chaw'd them, a moste barbarous worde for a moste barbarous Use. — Wh. we were Boyes, & he did yⁱˢ thinge, I was wont to trounce him Soundlie, but nowe had to contente Myselfe w. beatinge of him iii games of Billyardes in yᵉ Evg., & w. daringe of him to putt on yᵉ Gloves w. me, for Funne, wh. he mighte not doe, for I coude knocke him colde.

10th June.

Beinge gon to my Roome somewhatt earlie, for I found myselfe of a peevish humour, Clarence came to me, and pray'd a few minutes' Speache. — Sayde 't was

Love made him so Rude & Boysterous, he was privilie
betroth'd to his Cozen, Angelica Robertes, she whose
Father lives at Islipp, & colde not containe Himselfe
for Joye. — I sayinge, there was a Breache in yᵉ Familie,
he made Answer, 't was true, her Father & His, beinge
Cozens, did hate each other moste heartilie, butt for
him he cared not for that, & for Angelica, She gave
not a Continentall. — But, sayde I, Your Consideration
matters mightie Little, synce yᵉ Governours will not
heare to it. — He answered 't was for that he came to
me, I must be his allie, for reason of oure olde Friendᵖᵖ.
With that I had no Hearte to heare more, he made so
Light of suche a Division as parted me & my Happi-
nesse, but tolde him I was his Frend, wolde serve him
when he had Neede of me, & presentlie seeing my
Humour, he made excuse to goe, & left me to write
downe this, sicke in Mynde, and thinkinge ever of yᵉ
Woman who wil not oute of my Thoughtes for any
change of Place, neither of employe. — For indeede I
doe love Her moste heartilie, so yᵗ my Wordes can not
saye it, nor will yⁱˢ Booke containe it. — So I wil even
goe to Sleepe, yᵗ in my Dreames perchaunce my Fancie
maye do my Hearte better Service.

* 12ᵗʰ June.

She is here. — What Spyte is yⁱˢ of Fate & yᵉ alter'd
gods! That I, who mighte nott gett to see Her when
to See was to Hope, muste nowe daylie have Her in
my Sight, stucke lyke a fayre Apple under olde Tan-
talus his Nose. — Goinge downe to yᵉ Hotell to-day, for
to gett me some Tobackoe, was made aware yᵗ yᵉ Ffrench
familie had hyred one of yᵉ Cottages round-abouts. —

'T is a goodlie Dwellinge Without — Would I coude speake with as much Assurance of ye Innsyde!

13th June.

Goinge downe to ye Hotell againe To-day for more Tobackoe, sawe ye accursed name of W^mson on ye Registre. — Went about to a neighboringe Farm & satt me downe behynd ye Barne, for a ½ an Houre. — Frighted ye Horned Cattle w. talkinge to My Selfe.

15th June.

I wil make an Ende to y^is Businesse. — Wil make no onger Staye here. — Sawe Her to-day, driven Home fm. ye Beache, about 4½ of ye After-noone, by W^mson in his Dogge-Carte, wh. ye Cadde has broughten here. — Wil betake me to ye Boundlesse Weste — Not y^t I care aught for ye Boundlesse Weste, butt y^t I shal doe wel if haplie I leave my Memourie am^g ye Apaches & bringe Home my Scalpe.

16th June.

To Fyre Islande, in Winthrop's Yacht — ye Twinnes w. us, so Titteringe & Choppinge Laughter, y^t 't was worse y^n a Flocke of Sandpipers. — Found a grete Concourse of people there, Her amonge them, in a Suite of blue, y^t became Her bravelie. — She swimms lyke to a Fishe, butt everie Stroke of Her white Arms (of a lovelie Roundnesse) cleft, as 't were my Hearte, rather y^n ye Water. — She bow'd to me, on goinge into ye Water, w. muche Dignitie, & agayn on Cominge out, but y^is Tyme w. lesse Dignitie, by reason of ye Water in Her Cloathes, & Her Haire in Her Eyes. —

17th June.

Was for goinge awaie To-morrow, but Clarence cominge againe to my Chamber, & mightilie purswad-inge of me, I feare I am comitted to a verie sillie Undertakinge. — For I am promis'd to Help him secretlie to wedd his Cozen. — He wolde take no Deniall, wolde have it, his Brother car'd Naughte, 't was but ye Fighte of theyre Fathers, he was bounde it sholde be done, & 't were best I stoode his Witnesse, who was wel lyked of bothe ye Braunches of ye Family. — So 't was agree'd, y^t I shal staye Home to-morrowe fm. ye Expedition to Fyre Islande, feigning a Head-Ache, (wh. indeede I meante to do, in any Happ, for I cannot see Her againe,) & shall meet him at ye little Churche on ye Southe Roade. — He to drive to Islipp to fetch Angelica, lykewise her Witnesse, who sholde be some One of ye Girles, she hadd not yet made her Choice. — I made y^{is} Condition, it sholde not be either of ye Twinnes. — No, nor Bothe, for that matter. — Inquiringe as to ye Clergyman, he sayde ye Dominie was allreadic Squar'd.

New York, ye Buckingham Hotell, 19th June.

I am come to ye laste Entrie I shall ever putt downe in y^s Booke, and needes must y^t I putt it downe quick-lie, for all hath Happ'd in so short a Space, y^t my Heade whirles w. thynkinge of it. Y^e after-noone of Yester-daye, I set about Counterfeittinge of a Head-Ache, & so wel did I compasse it, y^t I verilie thinke one of y^e Twinnes was mynded to Stay Home & nurse me. — All havinge gone off, & Clarence on his waye to Islipp, I

sett forth for y^e Churche, where arriv'd I founde it
emptie, w. y^e Door open. — Went in & writh'd on y^o
hard Benches a $\frac{1}{4}$ of an Houre, when, hearinge a Sounde,
I look'd up & saw standinge in y^e Door-waye, Kathe-
rine Ffrench. — She seem'd muche astonished, saying
You Here! or y^e lyke. — I made Answer & sayde y^t
though my Familie were greate Sinners, yet had they
never been Excommunicate by y^e Churche. — She
sayde, they colde not Putt Out what never was in. —
While I was bethynkinge me wh. I mighte answer to
y^{ls}, she went on, sayinge I must excuse Her, She wolde
goe upp in ye Organ-Lofte. — I enquiring what for?
She sayde to practice on ye Organ. — She turn'd verie
Redd, of a warm Coloure, as She sayde this. — I ask'd
Do you come hither often? She replyinge Yes, I
enquir'd how ye Organ lyked Her. — She sayde Right
well, when I made question more curiously (for She
grew more Redd eache moment) how was ye Action?
ye Tone? how manie Stopps? Wh^{at} She growinge
gretelie Confus'd, I led Her into ye Churche, & show'd
Her y^t there was no Organ, y^t Choire beinge indeede a
Band, of i Tuninge-Forke, i Kitt, & i Horse-Fiddle. —
At this She fell to Smilinge & Blushinge att one Tyme.
— She perceiv'd our Errandes were ye Same, & crav'd
Pardon for Her Fibb. — I tolde Her, If She came
Thither to be Witness at her Frend's Weddinge, 'twas
no greate Fibb, 'twolde indeede be Practice for Her.
— This havinge a rude Sound, I added I thankt y^e
Starrs y^t had bro't us Together. She sayde if ye Starrs
appoint'd us to meete no oftener y^n this Couple shonde
be Wedded, She was wel content. This cominge on

me lyke a last Buffett of Fate, that She shoude so
despitefully intreate me, I was suddenlie Seized with
so Sorrie a Humour, & withal so angrie, y^t I colde
scarce Containe myselfe, but went & Sat downe neare
ye Doore, lookinge out till Clarence shd. come w. his
Bride. — Looking over my Sholder, I sawe y^t She
wente fm. Windowe to Windowe within, Pluckinge y^e
Blossoms fm. ye Vines, & settinge them in her Girdle.
— She seem'd most tall and faire, & swete to look
uponn, & itt Anger'd me ye More. — Meanwhiles, She
discours'd pleasantlie, asking me manie questions, to
the wh. I gave but shorte and churlish answers. She
ask'd Did I nott Knowe Angelica Roberts was Her
best Frend? How longe had I knowne of ye Betrothal?
Did I thinke 'twolde knitt ye House together, & Was
it not Sad to see a Familie thus Divided? — I answer'd
Her, I wd. not robb a Man of ye precious Righte to
Quarrell with his Relations. — And then, with medi-
tatinge on ye goode Lucke of Clarence, & my owne
harde Case, I had suche a sudden Rage of peevishness
y^t I knewe scarcelie what I did. — Soe when she ask'd
me merrilie why I turn'd my Backe on Her, I made
Reply I had turn'd my Backe on much Follie. — Wh.
was no sooner oute of my Mouthe than I was mightilie
Sorrie for it, and turninge aboute, I perceiv'd She was
in Teares & weepinge bitterlie. Wh^{at} my Hearte
wolde holde no More, & I rose upp & tooke Her in my
arms & Kiss'd & Comforted Her, She makinge no
Denyal, but seeminge greatlie to Neede such Solace,
wh. I was not Loathe to give Her. — Whiles we were
at This, onlie She had gott to Smilinge, & to sayinge

of Things which even y^is paper shal not knowe, came
in ye Dominie, sayinge He judg'd We were the Couple
he came to Wed. — With him ye Sexton & ye Sexton's
Wife. — My swete Kate, alle as roscy as Venus's Nape,
was for Denyinge of y^is, butt I wolde not have it, &
sayde Yes. — She remonstrating w. me, privilie, I
tolde Her She must not make me Out a Liar, y^t to
Deceave ye Man of God were a greavous Sinn, y^t I had
gott Her nowe, & wd. not lett her Slipp from me, &
did soe Talke Her Downe, & w. such Strengthe of
joie, y^t allmost before She knewe it, we Stoode upp, &
were Wed, w. a Ringe (tho' She Knewe it nott) wh.
belong'd to My G father. (Him y^t Cheated Her^n.) —

Wh was no sooner done, than in came Clarence &
Angelica, & were Wedded in theyre Turn. — The
Clergyman greatelie surprised, but more att ye Large-
ness of his Fee.

This Businesse being Ended, we fled by ye Trayne of
4½ o'cke, to y^is Place, where we wait till ye Bloode of
all ye Ffrenches have Tyme to coole downe, for ye wise
Mann who meeteth his Mother in Lawe ye 1st tyme, wil
meete her when she is Milde. —

And so I close y^is Journall, wh., tho' for ye moste
Parte 'tis but a peevish Scrawle, hath one Page of
Golde, wh^on I have writt ye laste strange Happ wh^by I
have layd Williamson by ye Heeles & found me y^e
sweetest Wife y^t ever

.　　　.　　　.

stopp'd a man's Mouthe w. kisses for writinge of
Her Prayses.

Stories by American Authors

MESSRS. CHARLES SCRIBNER'S SONS have in hand a publication of unusual importance and interest, in the volumes of "Stories by American Authors," of which they have just begun the issue.

The books carry their sufficient explanation in their brief title. They are collections of the more noteworthy short stories contributed by American writers during the last twenty-five years—and especially during the last ten—either to periodicals or publications now for some reason not easily accessible.

It is surprising that such a collection has not been attempted earlier, in view of the extraordinarily large proportion of strong work in American fiction which has been cast in the form of the short story.

If the publishers of the present collection are right, it will not only show the remarkably large number of contemporary American authors who have won general acknowledgment of their excellence in this field, but will surprise most readers by the number of capital and striking stories by less frequent writers, which are scattered through our recent periodical literature.

In England, in the well-known "Tales from Blackwood," the experiment was tried of publishing such stories taken from a single magazine within a limited time. But the noticeable feature of the present volumes will be seen to be the extent of the field from which they draw, and their fully representative character.

Cloth, 16mo, 50 cents each.

Stories by American Authors

The following is an alphabetical list of the stories contained in the first six volumes of the series which are now ready:

Balacchi Brothers, The. By Rebecca Harding Davis. Vol. I.

Brother Sebastian's Friendship. By Harold Frederic. Vol. VI.

Denver Express, The. By A. A. Hayes. Vol. VI.

Dinner Party, A. By John Eddy. Vol. II.

Documents in the Case, The. By Brander Matthews and H. C. Bunner. Vol. I.

End of New York, The. By Park Benjamin. Vol. V.

Friend Barton's Concern. By Mary Hallock Foote. Vol. IV.

Heartbreak Cameo, The. By Lizzie W. Champney. Vol. VI.

Inspired Lobbyist, An. By J. W. De Forest. Vol. IV.

Light Man, A. By Henry James. Vol. V.

Lost in the Fog. By Noah Brooks. Vol. IV.

Love in Old Cloathes. By H. C. Bunner. Vol. IV.

Martyr to Science, A. By Mary Putnam Jacobi, M.D. Vol. II.

Memorable Murder, A. By Celia Thaxter. Vol. III.

Miss Grief. By Constance Fenimore Woolson. Vol. IV.

Miss Eunice's Glove. By Albert Webster. Vol. VI.

Misfortunes of Bro' Thomas Wheatley, The. By Lina Redwood Fairfax. Vol. VI.

Mount of Sorrow, The. By Harriet Prescott Spofford. Vol. II.

Mrs. Knollys. By "J. S. of Dale." Vol. II.

Operation in Money, An. By Albert Webster. Vol. I.

Poor Ogla-Moga. By David D. Lloyd. Vol. III.

Sister Silvia. By Mary Agnes Tincker. Vol. II.

Spider's Eye, The. By Lucretia P. Hale. Vol. III.

Story of the Latin Quarter, A. By Frances Hodgson Burnett. Vol. III.

Tachypomp, The. By E. P. Mitchell. Vol. V.

Thirty Pieces, One of the. By W. H. Bishop. Vol. I.

Transferred Ghost, The. By Frank R. Stockton. Vol. II.

Two Buckets in a Well. By N. P. Willis. Vol. IV.

Two Purse Companions. By George Parsons Lathrop. Vol. III.

Venetian Glass. By Brander Matthews. Vol. III.

Village Convict, The. By C. H. White. Vol. VI.

Who was She? By Bayard Taylor. Vol. I.

Why Thomas was Discharged. By George Arnold. Vol. V.

Yatil. By F. D. Millet. Vol. V.

ATTRACTIVE BOOKS
IN PAPER COVERS.

GUERNDALE: An Old Story.

By J. S. OF DALE. 1 vol., 12mo, ... 50 cts.

NEWPORT: A Novel.

By GEORGE PARSONS LATHROP. 1 vol., 12mo, . . 50 cts.

JOHN BULL AND HIS ISLAND.

By MAX O'RELL. Eleventh thousand. 1 vol., 12mo, 50 cts.

LUTHER: A Short Biography.

By JAMES ANTHONY FROUDE, M.A. 1 vol., 12mo, . 30 cts.

OLD CREOLE DAYS.

By GEORGE W. CABLE. In two parts—each complete in itself—per volume, ... 30 cts.

MY HOUSE: An Ideal.

By O. B. BUNCE. 1 vol., 16mo, ... 50 cts.

RUDDER GRANGE.

By FRANK R. STOCKTON. 1 vol., 12mo, ... 60 cts.

SOCRATES.

A Translation of the Apology, Crito, and parts of the Phædo of Plato. New edition. 1 vol., 12mo, . 50 cts.

A DAY IN ATHENS WITH SOCRATES.

1 vol., 12mo, ... 50 cts.

MRS. BURNETT'S EARLIER STORIES.

LINDSEY'S LUCK, 30 cts. ; PRETTY POLLY PEMBERTON, 40 cts. ; KATHLEEN, 40 cts.; THEO, 30 cts.; MISS CRESPIGNY, 30 cts. Beautifully bound in ornamental paper covers.